"You wanted to see me . . . alone?"

Nicholas asked, a wicked smile spreading across his face.

Kate took an involuntary step back. "Close the door, please."

He complied and came farther into the room, his expression becoming serious. "Any reason in particular? You're not in trouble, are you?"

"No. But you are." She lifted the pistol in the air.

"Good God!" he exclaimed, a look of complete astonishment on his face. "What are you—"

"Damn you, sir! I won't let you steal my home away from me!"

"Steal—? Crestley Hall. I should have realized." Nicholas took a step closer, and she leveled the pistol at him. He paused, a grim smile coming to his face.

"Don't smile," she hissed angrily. "I mean to do this."

Other **Regency Romances**
from Avon Books

The Black Duke's Prize

SUZANNE ENOCH

AVON BOOKS ◆ NEW YORK

THE BLACK DUKE'S PRIZE is an original publication of Avon Books. This work has never before appeared in book form. This work is a novel. Any similarity to actual persons or events is purely coincidental.

AVON BOOKS
A division of
The Hearst Corporation
1350 Avenue of the Americas
New York, New York 10019

Copyright © 1995 by Suzanne Enoch
Published by arrangement with the author
Library of Congress Catalog Card Number: 94-96572
ISBN: 0-380-78052-6

First Avon Books Printing: May 1995

AVON TRADEMARK REG. U.S. PAT. OFF. AND IN OTHER COUNTRIES, MARCA REGISTRADA, HECHO EN U.S.A.

Printed in the U.S.A.

RA 10 9 8 7 6 5 4 3 2 1

To my sisters, Nancy and Cheryl,
for endless reading and for
laughing at all the right places—
I owe you each a quarter.

1

It was one thing to dream about being a lady in distress, Katherine Ralston had recently realized, and quite another entirely to be one. Particularly troubling was that a white knight, who never failed to make a timely appearance in fictional realms, was in this instance nowhere to be found. She would have to make do on her own, and though she was becoming accustomed to that idea, it did not make the circumstance any more pleasant or comforting.

" . . . so, you see, it's already done, m'dear. The passage was purchased a week ago." Simon Ralston looked up briefly from the papers he was shuffling across his late brother's dark-mahogany business desk and then lowered his head again when Kate made no reply. "All taken care of," he went on after a moment.

"I'm not leaving," Kate grumbled, her eyes focused on the rose-patterned carpet that she had played on as a child and her fists clenched so that she wouldn't be tempted to do any of the unladylike things she was contemplating. "This is my home."

"Well, m'dear, me being your guardian, as named by your dear father, it's mine for the next two years, and I'll run it as I see fit, thank you very much. And you won't

1

have any say anyway, young miss, because you are going to London, at the kind invitation of your godparents."

Kind and convenient, more like, Katherine thought bitterly. As soon as she was out the door Uncle Simon would likely sell off Crestley Hall piecemeal and pocket the profits. She had never liked her father's younger brother, and in the months since her mother's death her aversion had deepened to hatred. What had possessed her father to name Simon her guardian until her twenty-second birthday she couldn't imagine, though at the time the will had been drawn up the idea that Sir Richard Ralston would be killed in a carriage accident and his wife, Anne, would die of pneumonia two years later had seemed absurd. Now, however, Katherine found her home and her life in the hands of a man who would sell either for a good gambling stake.

He didn't even look like a Ralston, she decided as she stared at the wiry brown hair on top of his head, the only part of his face she could see now that his shuffling of papers had resumed. Both Kate and her father had the same fair complexion and wavy black hair as all the other Ralstons she had ever heard of. Her own tresses cascaded down to her waist when she brushed them out.

The one feature that her father and Simon did share was their brown eyes, so gentle and good-humored in her father and so stony in his brother. She herself, she thought thankfully, took after her mother's blue-eyed Irish ancestors, and the lack of resemblance between her and Uncle Simon had lately become something of a comfort. The less she had in common with him the better she liked it.

"You'd best take your sulks upstairs and finish packing, because I won't have another outburst of that damned temper of yours. Coach leaves first thing in the morning." Simon Ralston didn't even glance up this time.

After a moment of deliberate disobedience she stood and left the room. They had argued over her leaving several times during the past week, and she had known that nothing she said was going to change his mind. She had therefore completed what little of her packing there was to do. She was being sent away with what she could carry, and she more than doubted her uncle's word that the rest of her "necessities" would follow her to London.

Most of the servants had been let go during the course of the nine months since her uncle's arrival, a forced exodus that had begun as soon as her mother had become too ill to notice and Katherine too concerned over the Lady Anne's failing health to inform her of the doings. That night the house seemed even quieter than had become usual, and she wondered if its dead emptiness pressed on her uncle as it did on her. She dearly hoped so, but after a moment's reflection she doubted he would notice such a thing.

She had been to London only once before, when she had begun her Season two years earlier. The death of her father had ended the festivities after only a fortnight, and she didn't care if she ever went back again. Her current reason for going, as her uncle had made clear, was to get her away from Crestley. She wondered fleetingly if he had somehow arranged the invitation that had arrived a month ago from the Baron and Baroness of Clarey, her mother's dearest friends and her godparents, but swiftly brushed the thought away. The idea that Lord Neville or Lady Alison could be manipulated for even one moment by the likes of Uncle Simon was unthinkable, even to someone of her rather fanciful imagination.

It was Timms, one of the few remaining members of the staff, who scratched at her door the next morning to carry her baggage downstairs. The old butler lifted the two valises and turned toward the doorway, then stopped and cleared his throat. "Miss Kate?"

"Yes, Timms?" she responded, looking away reluctantly from what might be her last view out of her window at the failing gardens and the meadow and woods beyond.

"Take care, milady."

"Thank you, Timms," she responded, forcing a smile.

Downstairs she found her uncle waiting by the front door, and her spirits sank even further. She had hoped that he wouldn't bother to rise. She did not want her last sight of Crestley Hall to include him. There seemed to be no avoiding it, however, for though she passed by him without a word, he turned and followed her outside and down the front steps to the waiting hack.

She stopped and turned to face him, wishing she had inherited some of her father's height. "If one piece of furniture, one candlestick, one teacup is removed from Crestley Hall in my absence, I will carve the value of it out of your hide with my father's sword."

"You mind the Baron and Baroness like a good girl, Kate, and I might even inquire as to their working on trying to find you a husband, if anyone'd have a shrew like you." He pointed a finger at her. "Crestley Hall's a long way from London, and London's a bad place to be all on your own. You watch yourself."

Katherine stared at him for a moment, sudden uneasiness vying with her indignation and anger at his insult. If he meant his concluding words as a threat, it was the first time he had handed her one openly. He was up to something.

Timms handed her into the carriage. The hack would take her to the Red Boar Inn, where she would meet the mail stage to London. As they left the long drive she looked back at Crestley, already showing signs of the neglect her uncle had forced on it. And standing at the foot of the front steps, watching her out of sight, was Simon Ralston. Whatever he was planning, she would be back, and she would claim what was hers.

2

"**A**nother hand, Sommesby," Francis DuPres demanded, leaning forward and digging the pads of his fingers into the wood table.

Unmoved by the plea, Nicholas Varon, Duke of Sommesby, continued his push away from the gaming table and stood. "Sorry, gentlemen, but despite rumors to the contrary, occasionally even I need sleep."

"Sleep has nothing to do with your taking your winnings and leaving."

"No, I don't believe it does." His gray eyes holding DuPres's close-set brown ones, he plucked a chip out of the pile and flipped it at the other man without bothering to check its value. "My compliments."

Beside him Thomas Elder, the Viscount of Sheresford, chuckled. "Quit complaining, DuPres. That chip's worth more than you won all evening." He scooped what remained of his evening's losses into his own hand. "Any of those for me?" he asked, gesturing at the substantial pile before Nicholas.

Stifling a yawn that wasn't entirely feigned, Nicholas summoned one of the clerks to cash him in. "Not a chance, Thomas," he retorted with a smile. "And I'm hoping this will serve to dissuade you from wasting your blunt on that brown nag you've been eyeing." He straightened

5

his cravat with its black onyx pin, then flicked an imaginary speck of dust off the sleeve of his black jacket.

"I think 'not a chance' is a rather accurate description of the evening," DuPres commented.

Nicholas stiffened. "Care to explain that remark?" he said quietly, wondering if he was on his way to setting a record for trouble this Season. Two days before, he had rather spectacularly parted ways with the exquisitely devious Josette Bettreaux, and now this. The Season was new, the nights at White's still slow and lazy. DuPres had been an unwelcome participant in what had been a friendly game of faro, and now for some reason it appeared that he wished to test the rumors about the Varon black temper. Nicholas was more than willing to oblige.

"You know what I'm talking about." Francis DuPres got to his feet, apparently overconfident, or drunk, enough to press the issue.

"Don't be a fool." Captain Reg Hillary, second of four sons in the prolific Hillary family, placed a hand on DuPres's shoulder and tried to push him back into his seat.

When DuPres remained standing, Nicholas set his gloves down again and leaned his knuckles into the table. "Make the accusation, then," he murmured. Those who knew him would have recognized the danger signs of the quiet voice and the gray eyes that now flashed with emerald highlights. Thomas did, for he stepped back from the table. Reg likewise removed himself from Francis's side. The sound in the crowded gaming hall died as the other patrons turned to view the excitement. DuPres paled, but held his ground.

"You've lost barely a hand all evening, Sommesby," the small man whined. He glanced about, to find everyone staring at him. "I don't see why anyone should be surprised." He looked back at Nicholas. "Everyone knows your repu—"

The rest of his sentence was lost as Nicholas planted a fist full into his face. DuPres went backward over his chair, crashed into the table behind that, and ended up sprawled on the floor with the contents of several drinks doing various degrees of damage to his jacket and garish gold waistcoat. He likely wasn't aware of the results of his fall, for he was plainly unconscious, blood welling from his lip and making his already pasty features look even more pale.

"Damn me," Thomas muttered with something like awe in his voice as he looked down at DuPres's crumpled form. "One punch."

Nicholas looked around the room, his eyes narrowed. No one else came forward to confront him. As he watched his fellow patrons eyeing him warily, a dark, cynical smile touched his lips. Unless he misjudged badly, which he rarely did, no one would be accusing him of anything for a while.

He flipped a chip of excessive value at the club's nervous manager, watching the man's expression ease, and then another onto DuPres's chest. "Should cover the cost of replacing that rag," he murmured. When he turned to leave, Thomas followed.

The other patrons of White's stepped aside, and then he and Thomas were out in the cold predawn air. His residence was only a short walk away and so he waved his coach on, preferring to walk off his mood and the considerable amount of liquor he had consumed. The viscount hesitated a moment before he followed.

"You shouldn't have done that," Sheresford commented, tucking his hands into the armpits of his dark brown jacket.

"Shouldn't I have?" Nicholas responded.

"DuPres might act like a fool, Nick, but he's a cunning sort. Now you've insulted him twice over."

"Didn't look so cunning lying there on the floor." Nicholas looked over at the younger man. "And I was not going to let him get away with saying that about me."

"He fancies himself a nonesuch. Now everyone'll be laughing at him."

"He's a fop with about as much fashion sense as I have skill with a needle."

Grinning, Thomas placed a hand on Nicholas's shoulder. "I've heard you've mended a tear or two in an emergency." He glanced down at Nicholas's splendid superfine jacket. "We can't all be you," he said ruefully.

This time Nicholas laughed aloud, though he deliberately chose to misread the viscount's remark. "Thank Lucifer for that."

"Bah," Thomas spat out, scowling. "I don't know why I bother."

"Neither do I," Nicholas returned, and resumed his long-strided walk. "I don't recall ever encouraging you."

"Why don't you listen to me once in a while?" Thomas continued, though he made no move to follow.

"I'm not hiring for a conscience at the moment, Thomas, but I'll let you know if I do," he said over his shoulder, not bothering to slow his pace.

"You've made an enemy of DuPres, Nick. Be careful."

This time Nicholas ignored him completely.

"Damn you, Varon," Thomas called out, and turned back to his own coach.

"Too late," Nicholas retorted under his breath, and continued on alone in the dark.

Nicholas arose earlier than he would have liked the next morning, driven from sleep both by the pounding of his skull and by the loud squabbling of a pair of carriage drivers who had apparently collided in the street below. He summoned his valet and dressed, then made his way downstairs for a cup of tea.

The sound of the front door opening came to his ears as he settled into the chair in his study to go through the previous day's mail and write his regrets to most of the invitations he had received. Briefly he wondered how many hostesses would wish they had not sent them out after hearing of the second scandal he had caused. It seemed, though, that the worse the spectacle the more invitations he received. With a sigh he glanced up at the clock on the mantel. Nine o'clock in the morning on the fifth day of the Season, and he was again a disgrace to the family name.

"Nicky, you're a disgrace."

Nicholas turned to look at the petite, dark-haired woman standing in the doorway. Julia Varon was, as always, beautifully attired, this morning in a light-green muslin that served to bring out the emerald highlights in her dark-gray eyes. "You look fetching, Mama," he responded, rising.

She waved a hand at him. "Fetching is for those pretty young things you cause so much misery. I believe I have matured to the point of being what is called 'elegant.' "

"You look elegant, Mama," Nicholas amended, grinning in the way that had become famous for setting fetching hearts fluttering.

"Mon dieu, Nicky, will you never outgrow this desire to cause trouble?" She poured herself a cup of tea from the tray that had magically appeared almost simultaneously with her arrival, and sat in one of the chairs before the fire.

"I didn't cause the trouble this time," he retorted, leaning over the back of the chair to kiss her on the cheek. "I was merely defending the family name."

"And Josette Bettreaux?"

Nicholas straightened, and turned toward the window. "That wasn't my fault either."

"No?"

"No. I didn't send her out to find some schoolboy and encourage him to shoot me. That was all her idea." In fact, if he had known what kind of plot that devious female would cook up to try to arouse his jealousy that night, he would have stayed at home.

His mother frowned at him and added a small teaspoon of sugar to her tea. "A little early to be drinking, yes?"

He glanced down to see that he was fiddling with the decanter of brandy at his elbow. Misreading him was unusual for her, but she was likely furious at him to begin with. "Anything else?" he asked quietly, annoyed, and deliberately lifted the decanter to pour himself a drink. He took a swallow, gazing at her over the snifter's rim and daring her to comment further.

"That DuPres, now that you've humiliated him, you aren't going to call him out and kill him, are you?" Though Julia Varon spoke English flawlessly, she still tended to arrange her sentences in the manner of her native France. That did not mean that she couldn't be as direct and to the point as anyone Nicholas had ever cared to meet.

"I remember when you would have been concerned over *my* well-being," he answered.

"That was when you were concerned," she responded with deceptive mildness, sipping at her tea.

"I think DuPres's learned his lesson. And since I've encouraged Josette to take a holiday in France, I believe she will become enlightened as well."

"Mon dieu, however could you have chosen such a one as that, anyway? She has no honor at all."

"I do not believe this to be a subject one discusses with one's mother." He drained the snifter and refilled it, knowing that would annoy her even further.

"Someone has to discuss it with you. You've frightened away everyone else whose advice you could trust."

At that he turned, raising an eyebrow in mock surprise. "I haven't frightened anyone into anything."

"You forget, I lived with that temper for thirty years, in your father. I know how it is. You have a way when you are angry that frightens people. And you are afraid to trust those you could."

He sat in the chair opposite her and held the brandy up. Instead of drinking, he swirled the amber liquid, examining it against the firelight. He knew he had a temper, and he knew that, like his father, he tended to use it as a weapon to keep the people around him at a distance.

"Nicky, you could do so much better than the likes of Josette Bettreaux," his mother said quietly. "Don't you realize that?"

"Is that why you came here, to show me my sins and attempt to marry me off?" Nicholas took another swallow, enjoying the light, burning sensation as the liquid traveled down his throat. "Who is it this time? I saw you talking with the Marchioness of Belning the other night, before all hell broke loose. Is it her simpering daughter—what's her name, Azalea?"

"Althaea," his mother retorted. "Have you ever even spoken to her?"

"I tried to, last year. Chit looked as though she wanted to faint."

Julia became occupied with her tea for a moment. "You can be a bit—how shall I say—intimidating," she finally responded, unable to stifle her smile.

"Well, I can't very well have a wife who becomes unconscious every time I set eyes on her. Besides, in the bare minute we conversed I believe we covered everything we had in common."

This time his mother's chuckle was audible. Abruptly she sobered. "You're almost thirty, Nicky. When?" Julia put her cup aside and sat forward in her chair, catching his dark-gray eyes with her own.

"Maybe never," he replied, and abruptly stood and strode toward the window again, more uncomfortable than was usual with the familiar line of questions. He had thought about marriage from time to time, but it and his temperament and style of living simply did not seem to be in any way compatible. "Don't you ever consider that letting the Varon black temper dwindle out of existence might be doing society a favor?"

The Dowager Duchess stood as well, facing his six-foot height squarely, as though she weren't a full foot shorter than he. "Never say that, Nicholas. You insult yourself, you insult your father, and you insult me."

He immediately regretted the words. He hadn't meant to offend her, but had only been trying to express what he had been feeling more and more strongly of late. "You don't have the black blood, Mama," he responded evenly.

"I fell in love with it," she answered softly.

He knew she still deeply mourned John Varon, though her husband had been gone for nearly eight years now. Silently he closed the distance between them and leaned over her hand to kiss her knuckle. "I do suppose London would be sadly flat without us," he conceded. He and his father had been too much alike to get along well, but there were times when he sorely missed the old duke.

She nodded, smiling, and tightened her grip on his fingers. "Please try to avoid Josette and DuPres for a time, will you?"

"No," he answered, freeing his hand. "I'll not hide from that woman or that fool." Her look darkened, and he went on without pause. "If they wish to avoid me, however, I shall not seek them out."

She nodded again. "Thank you, Nicky."

He bowed elegantly, then seated himself again. "You know as well as I, though, if it's not one of them, it will be someone else. It always is. It's one of my main talents, angering people."

"You shouldn't practice it so much," she replied.

3

Katherine stood looking up at Hampton House. It was as large as Crestley, and her godparents also owned the grand Clarey estate, several days to the west. She had no idea why they would want her to stay with them, goddaughter or no. It abruptly occurred to her that they might not even be in town. She wasn't aware of whether her uncle had sent them a firm date for her arrival or not, and as she had been hoping somehow to avoid coming to London, she hadn't notified them either. They might very well have given up on her and left on another of their exotic travels.

Well, she wouldn't find out by waiting in the street. She picked up her heavy valises, squared her shoulders, and walked up to the front door. Setting one of the bags down, she reached out and firmly swung the intricately tooled brass knocker against the door. With the sound still echoing, the door swung open. She found herself looking up into the sternest, thinnest face she had ever seen.

"Yes?" the butler prompted after a moment.

"I am Katherine Ralston," she said, dismayed that her voice broke in the face of the man's stare. "I am here to see the Hamptons."

"The baron and baroness are not in this evening," the butler replied. He looked down at her valises and then back at her face. "I suggest you call again in the morning." He began to close the door.

At least they were in town. "Wait," Katherine protested, fighting abrupt panic at the thought of being left on her own in London at night. "My mother was Lady Anne Ralston, an old friend of the Hamptons. They invited me to come here . . . and I have nowhere else to stay this evening."

He nodded, acknowledging that he had heard of her mother, but still did not move aside. She knew that she must look ridiculous, standing outside with her bags and arguing with this impossibly tall person, and she began to grow angry.

"Are you going to let me in?" she asked, stamping her foot.

"I am inclined not to," he replied.

"Tell me this, then," she countered. "Are the baron and baroness more likely to hand you your papers for letting a stranger in to wait for them in their hall or for putting the daughter of one of their dearest friends out into the street?"

The butler blinked. "I see your point," he finally said, and she thought she heard amusement in his voice. "This way, Miss Ralston."

He stepped aside, and, chin up, she walked past him into the elegant hall. The open door off to the left must have been the library, for she caught a glimpse of a shelf lined with books. In front of her the main staircase turned once and led to a balcony, behind which she could see more doors. The hall widened out to the right past the door to the sitting room, and it was to this shallow alcove that the butler gestured her. She sat on the narrow bench, her valises on the floor beside her.

"I will have someone bring you a cup of tea," the butler said, and then turned away. Before he passed out of sight he looked back over his shoulder. "My name is Rawlins, if you should require anything further."

"Thank you, Rawlins," she answered, and with a small nod he disappeared into the depths of the house.

She had arrived, though not nearly in the manner she had anticipated. At least the hallway was warmer than the night air outside, and after a maid had brought her a cup of hot, strong tea she began to feel more composed. Even with the master and mistress gone from the house it seemed more alive than Crestley had for years. In the background she could hear occasional quiet conversation, and pots and pans rattled in the kitchen as servants cleaned up for the night.

She had hardly realized she was sleepy, before she was awakened by the sound of the front door opening. Rawlins stood there accepting the outer garments of the couple entering the house. Katherine shot to her feet as Rawlins gestured in her direction.

"My lord, this young lady arrived earlier this evening, claiming to be one Katherine Ralston. I thought it best she wait here for your return."

Katherine ignored his somewhat prejudiced version of events as Lady Alison spun around, her blue silk skirts rustling. Light-blue eyes widened as they took her in, and Katherine self-consciously smoothed out the simple material of her own dull, well-traveled dress.

"Kate?"

"Yes, Lady Alison. I'm sorry not to have written that I was coming." Before she could say anything else the plump blond woman swept forward to embrace her.

Katherine's uncertainty over whether she would be welcomed vanished as Lord Neville stepped up and put a hand on his wife's shoulder. "My turn, Alice." In a moment he was embracing her as well. "You are the image of your mother, Kate."

"We were so sorry to learn of Anne's death," Lady Alison said quietly, taking her hand. "I wish we had been there for you. We should never have gone to Spain."

Kate nodded, half in tears at their unexpected kindness. "You couldn't have known."

Lord Neville seemed to realize her distress, for he cleared his throat and motioned at Rawlins, standing inconspicuously in the background. "Rawlins, have Miss Ralston's bags taken upstairs to the green room and the bed made ready."

"Yes, m'lord." The butler bent his long frame and lifted the valises himself, then headed up the stairs and vanished into one of the rooms.

"Come into the drawing room." Lady Alison, still holding Katherine's hand tightly, led her through one of the doors off the main hall.

The room was large and comfortable, with two long couches placed at right angles to each other on a huge Persian carpet. Ornaments and knickknacks from several different countries and cultures decorated the walls, mantel, and tables. Lady Alison brought her to the nearest couch and sat her down, taking a place beside her. Lord Neville followed a few moments later and took one of the chairs by the fire, which crackled in the intricately carved fireplace.

"How was your trip here?" Lady Alison asked.

"I'm a little tired," Kate confessed, bringing her eyes back to the baroness from her perusal of an African wood carving. "The stage was delayed by a dairy herd this afternoon, and the walls of the inn last night were so thin, I had to listen to the squire next door snoring all night."

"The stage?" the baron exclaimed. "Why didn't your uncle send you in your own coach, or hire a private one for you? The mail stage is no place for a lady."

Katherine flinched at the indignation in his voice. She had no wish to pour out all of her troubles immediately upon her arrival. "Uncle Simon thought it best," she muttered, angry again at this latest insult her uncle had handed her. "And I didn't come here to burden you with my problems." Even with her gaze set on the floor, she sensed the look that passed between the baron and his wife.

"Kate, would it make any difference if I said that, while I always had and always shall bear great affection for your father, I never could countenance that wretched brother of his?"

"Neville!" Lady Alison reprimanded.

"Neither could I," Katherine responded feelingly. She grimaced. "I mean to handle this on my own," she stated as a preface, looking down at her toes, "but now that I am here I suppose you should be made aware of the circumstances."

And so she told them, beginning with her mother's illness and her uncle's timely—or so it had seemed—arrival, and proceeding to the provisions of her father's will, which were disclosed upon her mother's death. After a hesitation she told them of her suspicions concerning Uncle Simon's plans for Crestley and her present inability to do anything about it.

"The scoundrel," Lady Alison breathed when Katherine had finished the tale. "What are we to do?"

"I mean to handle it myself," Katherine repeated firmly. "I only told you because you have been so kind."

" 'Kind' has nothing to do with it, child. Your mother was my closest friend, and I loved her dearly. You are her daughter, and I love you as well. Whatever happens to Crestley Hall, our home is yours. You are our daughter now."

Again tears came to Kate's eyes. "Thank you both," she managed to say brokenly.

Lady Alison patted her hand. "You must be exhausted, child. I'll show you to your bedchamber." The baroness stood, pulling Katherine up after her, and led her from the room.

Katherine felt completely spent, and could barely keep her eyes open as they climbed the stairs. The room Alison showed her was decorated in greens and whites and lit by a small, cheerful fire. As she looked around the chamber Katherine realized that tears had begun flowing down her face.

"Are you all right?" the baroness asked, putting a hand on her shoulder.

Katherine nodded. "I only just realized how good it is to be with friends again," she said with a sigh.

"We let you stay away far too long," Alison murmured, hugging her again. "Shall I send my maid to you?"

"No, I can do for myself," Katherine answered, nearly crossing her eyes in an effort to keep them open.

Lady Alison nodded. "Sleep well, Kate." She smiled, and leaned over to kiss Katherine on the cheek. "And have no worries. You may stay with Neville and me for as long as you wish."

After two full days of shopping and sightseeing, Katherine very nearly felt like her old self. Lady Alison had secured an invitation for her to join them at the Albey ball, and she looked forward to it with some excitement. There hadn't been much occasion for her to dance lately. Hampton House was beautiful, and it reminded her of Crestley in the old days, before her father's death. The danger now was that she would find it so pleasant that she would forget the damage probably even at that moment being done to her home. She renewed her vow that she would let no harm come to Crestley, and she sent off a determinedly friendly letter to her uncle, mostly to see if he would respond.

She was surprised and pleased to discover that Lord Neville had hired a maid for her. The first gown she and Lady Alison had ordered arrived from the dressmaker's, and just before dusk she summoned Emmie to help her dress. That accomplished, she seated herself at the dressing table while the maid attempted to draw her hair back to fasten it in a bun at her neck.

"Miss Kate," the slim, brown-eyed girl stated after several minutes of struggling, "your hair seems to have a mind of its own. I get one part up and the other side escapes."

"I know." Katherine sighed. "I can never get it to do what I want." Lately she had settled for jamming a bonnet down over it and hoping that no one would notice the straying strands.

"Well, let's try something else, then." Emmie picked up the two silver clips they had purchased the day before and pulled the sides back with them. The rest of Katherine's hair cascaded down her back in a heavy black waterfall, through which Emmie wove a thin silver ribbon. Finally the maid stepped back. "My," she breathed after a moment. "I think you'll do fine."

Katherine turned to look full into the mirror, and was startled by what she saw. She had dressed in finery before, but for perhaps the first time in her life she felt beautiful. The dark blue in the gown exactly matched the color of her eyes, and her skin seemed to glow with the sudden rush of excitement that ran through her.

"Emmie," she said, sitting straighter, "that brown box in the top dresser drawer—will you bring it to me, please?"

The maid did as she was bid, and Katherine opened the lid to pull out a single strand of milky-white pearls. They had been her mother's, and Emmie sighed again as she helped Katherine fasten them around her neck.

"That's perfection, Miss Kate," she said, dimpling.

"Well, I don't know about that, but thank you."

When she made her way downstairs a few moments later Katherine was greeted with similar words from her godparents. Tears formed in Lady Alison's eyes, and Kate rushed over to her. "What is it?"

Her godmother took her hand and squeezed it. "Nothing, child. It's just that you look so like your mother. You are a beauty."

Lord Neville cleared his throat. "Come, ladies. I will be the envy of every man present tonight, for the two most beautiful women in London arrive with me."

Twenty-five minutes later, Lord Neville was introducing Katherine to Lord James Albey and his wife, Cassia, their host and hostess for the evening. And then, her hand on Lord Neville's arm, she was led into the ballroom. She had received permission to waltz during her truncated Season, and Lady Alison had procured a dance card for her, but as she knew no one she didn't hold much hope that she would be asked onto the floor. Instead she stood with her godparents watching the crowded room and the dancers stepping gracefully about the highly polished floor.

"Alison."

Katherine turned when Alison did, to face the voice. A petite, dark-haired woman dressed in an elegant emerald gown approached them, a smile on her face. "Julia," Alison responded warmly, and grasped the small woman's outstretched hands. "I missed you at Vauxhall last week."

The woman laughed. "When was the last time you did see me at Vauxhall, eh?"

The accent was faintly French, and Katherine looked at her curiously. As though sensing the attention, the woman turned to face her. Katherine was struck by the unusual dark-gray eyes that seemed to hold emerald highlights.

"Who is your friend, Alison?"

"Who does she remind you of?" Lady Alison responded, urging Katherine forward.

The scrutiny made Katherine a bit uncomfortable, for she had the abrupt impression that the woman saw a great deal more than she might have wished. After a moment the gray eyes widened. "Anne Ralston's daughter?" she asked, and Katherine nodded.

"Kate, may I present the Duchess of Sommesby? Julia Varon, Katherine Ralston."

"I believe the correct term is 'Dowager Duchess,' " Julia corrected with a good-humored frown.

"I am pleased to meet you, Your Grace," Katherine said with a smile, curtseying.

The Dowager Duchess smiled at her, then stiffened as her eyes shifted to someone approaching them from behind. "Pah, it is that *chien*, Francis DuPres."

Curious at the duchess's offended tone, Katherine turned to face the short man approaching them. If they hadn't been at a gathering of London's *haut ton*, she would have thought him some sort of street performer, for he was clothed in a garish yellow jacket and waistcoat, while his breeches were a light lime green. The points of his shirt were nearly high enough to cover his ears, and he had an ugly purple bruise on his chin.

"Clarey," the man said with a nod at Lord Neville, then turned his close-set brown eyes on the duchess. "Your Grace," he drawled, his tone insulting.

"Go away, little man," she replied, and Alison sucked in her breath.

The tension around them abruptly escalated, and others were beginning to look their way. "Please forgive my forwardness, Baroness," the man said to Alison, ignoring the duchess, "but I simply had to know who this lovely creature was." With that he reached out to take Katherine's hand and brushed it with his lips.

Alison glanced over at the duchess, who shrugged, her lips tight. "Mr. DuPres, my goddaughter, Katherine Ralston. Kate, Mr. Francis DuPres."

"Miss Ralston, I am delighted to meet you."

"Thank you," Kate replied, trying to tug her hand free without being obvious about it.

"Now will you go away?" the duchess hissed.

"Not until our charming Miss Ralston agrees to grant me this dance," DuPres replied, looking at Katherine expectantly.

Kate didn't know what to do. What little she had seen of this man she didn't like, and she had no wish to insult Julia Varon, but neither did she want to be in the middle of the shouting match that she sensed might erupt if DuPres and the Dowager Duchess remained in close proximity. Abruptly the empty dance card was pulled out of her hand.

"Sorry, DuPres," an unfamiliar male voice said from behind her, "this dance is mine."

Katherine turned quickly to see a tall, raven-haired man scrutinizing her dance card. He glanced over at her speculatively with dark-gray eyes that held green highlights, much like Julia Varon's. He was broad-shouldered and lean and was dressed all in black, from his top boots to his exquisitely tailored jacket, with only a foamy white cravat and shirt to contrast the starkness. The effect was strikingly handsome, as was the man who affected it.

"Yes, 'fraid so, DuPres, my name's first." The stranger looked down to further examine the card, again giving her a quick, unreadable glance. "In fact, I don't see your name here at all."

"I have requested a dance," DuPres spat out, and reached for the card.

The stranger returned it smoothly to Kate. "So sorry, then. Her card's full, and you're not on it." Before she could say a word, he took her hand and led her onto the dance floor as the orchestra struck up a waltz.

Whoever her rescuer was, he was a graceful dancer. It took a moment for what had happened to sink in, it had all occurred so quickly. One moment she was trying to find a way to avoid dancing with Francis DuPres, and the next she was waltzing with a complete stranger.

"Thank you," she said after a moment.

The eyes that had been gazing across the floor shifted back to her. "For what?"

"I had no desire to dance with him." She glanced over to where DuPres stood glaring at them. There was an empty space around him, as though no one wanted to be associated with him.

"I didn't do it for you," he responded rudely, looking away again, his expression bored. "I did it to save my mother from embarrassment."

He was Julia Varon's son, then, as she had suspected. "Which was why I didn't want to dance with Mr. DuPres myself," she noted, for the moment ignoring his lack of manners.

The unusual eyes returned to her. "What is your name?" he drawled.

"Katherine Ralston," she replied. "And yours?" She had been hearing more than enough rumors since her arrival in

London to be fairly certain of his identity, but he should at least have had the courtesy to introduce himself.

"Nicholas Varon," he answered promptly. "What is your relationship to Neville and Alison Hampton?"

"They are my godparents," she replied, trying to keep from staring at him. This was the Black Duke of Sommesby she was dancing with, who had knocked out someone, probably Francis DuPres, at White's, and who had nearly started a duel in someone's ballroom over his mistress. Her maid had mentioned other things, which at the moment she was too rattled to recall.

"And how do you know Francis DuPres?" he pursued, either not noticing or ignoring her discomfiture.

"I only met him five minutes ago," she answered, the aloof, direct questions and the light, skillful touch of his hand on the small of her back beginning to annoy her despite her trepidation. "What is your relationship to Mr. DuPres?"

"None of your business," he said flatly, looking away again.

That wasn't very polite, and neither was the way he kept looking about the room, barely paying attention to her or to the dance. "It was quite insightful of me to include your name at the top of my dance card, don't you think?" she asked, her Irish temper beginning to flare.

Once again the eyes met hers, and this time she thought she saw a brief look of appreciation touch them. It was gone before she could be certain. "Indeed it was. Quite impressive."

"Yes," she agreed. "I only hope the rest of my choices are as impressive."

"Miss Ralston, I really don't care who you find to fill the remainder of your dance card," he said, apparently tiring completely of his role as rescuer. "I told you my reasons for bringing you out here."

"Of course, Your Grace," she answered, with admirable calm, she thought. "But, you see, while your problem has been solved, mine remains. I still do not wish to dance with Mr. DuPres, and you have informed him that I will be partnered for the entire evening. You have made one of us into a liar."

"Good God," he muttered under his breath. Apparently she had his attention now. "Don't you wish to speak about the weather or the latest Paris fashion or some such thing?"

"No."

The music ended, and she turned away from him to join in the general applause as he rather abruptly released her. Lady Alison beckoned to her from the far side of the room, and she started over. She had taken no more than a step or two when her hand was taken and tucked around a strong, black-clothed forearm.

"One does not leave one's dance partner if one wishes to avoid a scandal, Miss Ralston," Varon murmured, taking the lead as they headed off the floor.

"I wasn't aware that my doings concerned you," she responded hotly, a little surprised that he would care whether she caused a scandal or not.

Lady Alison wore an expression of slight uneasiness as they approached, but she smiled readily enough at the duke. "They are about to serve supper," she explained. "Nick, thank you for your assistance."

Varon glanced down at Kate, then back at the baroness. "It was my pleasure," he said smoothly, making Katherine wish to stomp on his foot.

Lord Neville joined them, and Kate found herself, to her annoyed chagrin, being escorted into the dining hall by the Black Duke. The seats had been assigned beforehand by the hostess, and Sommesby brought her to her chair and helped her into it, then leaned over her shoulder.

"Give me your card," he murmured.

She half turned to look at him. "What?"

"A good turn deserves a good turn. Give me your dance card, Miss Ralston." He touched her elbow under the level of the table, and after a hesitation she slipped the card into his hand.

During supper most of the other women at the table took at least a moment to glance in her direction, and she could almost see the speculation and curiosity, not all of it friendly. Belatedly she wondered what kind of favor the Duke of Sommesby had done for her. He sat close to the head of the table, and was receiving far more attention than she. She wanted no scandal attached to her, for she was only there to bide her time until she could return to Crestley.

Halfway through the meal she turned from conversing with Squire John Delgood of Berkshire and glanced over to see the Black Duke's eyes on her. She blushed and quickly looked away. Whatever had possessed her to bait him, she certainly now regretted the action. As she composed herself over supper, she had time to remember a great deal more of Emmie's stories concerning the Black Duke. There were rumors that he had killed or wounded several men in duels, and because of an argument, he had purposely gambled the Viscount of Worton out of his entire estate and had then turned around and handed the deed to the nearest footman, which had caused a second scandal. And now he had been her first dance partner at her first ball after her return to London.

Supper ended, and the guests drifted either upstairs to the gaming tables or back into the ballroom. She looked about, but didn't see the duke or her dance card anywhere. Likely he had gone to gamble and taken it with him. She began to curse him under her breath. Then, sensing someone behind her, she turned to see him standing there, looking down at her.

"A pleasure again, Miss Ralston," he said, and bent to kiss her hand. As he released it, her card was slipped expertly back into her palm. He then took Lady Alison's hand as well, granting her a slight smile, and headed out toward the stairs.

Katherine turned the card over in her hand. It was filled with names. Her godmother looked over at it as well and gave a surprised smile.

"He's partnered you with some of the most respected, and interesting, members of the *ton*. However did you convince him to assist you?"

Katherine shrugged, her eyes on the last name on the card. The bold lettering read only "N. Varon."

4

The Duke of Sommesby spent only a short time upstairs, for the games were woefully tame, and the company even more so. Aside from that, by filling her dance card he had in a manner put himself in the role of Miss Ralston's host, and he wished to see how she was enjoying her evening. He entered the ballroom again and lounged against the back wall to watch.

At that moment she was engaged in a country dance with the Viscount of Sheresford. Thomas appeared to be pleased, for he smiled as he spoke. She laughed in response, and Nicholas noted again that despite her rather haphazard manners she was quite attractive. The silver ribbons in her long black hair glowed in the candlelight, and the simple blue gown showed off her slim figure admirably.

"Nick?"

Neville Hampton approached from the chairs lining one side of the room, and Nicholas pushed himself upright away from the wall. "Neville," he said, shaking the older man's hand and wondering if he was about to be warned away from the baron's goddaughter. Clarey had little to worry about, however, for schoolroom misses held little interest for Nicholas.

Instead Neville mimed a punch. "Congratulations on the

flusher you handed Francis DuPres. Anyone knows any-thing about you, they know you're no cheat." Nicholas in-clined his head but said nothing, preferring to forget the entire incident and Francis DuPres. Clarey seemed to real-ize this, for he nodded and stepped closer. "Will you call on me tomorrow morning? There is something I wish to discuss with you."

Nicholas nodded, somewhat surprised that the baron would seek his counsel. "I'll be there, Neville."

A country dance was followed by a quadrille; he was not particularly fond of either. He watched as Captain Reg Hillary was introduced to Miss Ralston and led her out onto the floor. With a curse that had the women closest to him looking at him warily, he realized that his heroic ef-forts to keep Miss Ralston from being the object of scan-dal would fail if the Black Duke claimed her for the first and last dance of the evening and partnered no one else in between. With a put-upon sigh at what he was having to go through, all because she had called him on his actions—the ungrateful chit—he sought out his mother. The duchess was seated again beside the Marchioness of Belning, the two of them no doubt deep in conversation about how to trap him into matrimony.

"Mama, dance with me," he said, holding out his hand.

With a surprised look she rose and allowed herself to be led out onto the floor. "A quadrille, Nicky?" she mur-mured.

He ignored her comment, and instead spent most of the time watching Miss Ralston and Reg. Once again she was smiling, and he noted that he was not the only one looking her way. After the quadrille ended he escorted his mother back to her seat. The orchestra struck up a waltz, and he spied Azalea, no, Althaea Hillary cowering on the far side of the marchioness. Sighing again, he stopped before her. "May I have this dance, Miss Hillary?"

She blanched, but the marchioness smiled at him and el-bowed her daughter in the side. With a murmured word that he assumed to be an affirmative, the girl rose. When an opening presented itself he swept her out onto the floor.

"Are you having a pleasant evening, Miss Hillary?" he asked after a moment, eyeing the top of her auburn hair, as her eyes were apparently occupied with staring at his boots.

She lifted her head, nearly knocking him in the chin, and stammered something that he again assumed to be an affirmative. There was nothing wrong with Althaea Hillary physically; on the contrary, she was quite attractive, with long, curling lashes and soft brown doe's eyes that young men inclined toward such things wrote poetry about. If only she had had the power of speech, and something to say if she could speak, he might have found her tolerably pleasant. He couldn't help but note the vast difference between Althaea Hillary and the outspoken Miss Ralston, though he couldn't say which of the two he found more taxing.

"How are you enjoying the Season so far?" he ventured, curious to see how she would react to a question to which she couldn't answer yes or no.

"Qut 'll, nk you," came out of her mouth in an almost voiceless whisper, and Nicholas shut his eyes for just a moment.

"Beg pardon?" he said, leaning closer.

"Quite well, thank you," she managed to articulate, glancing up at his face.

Feeling as though he had accomplished something of a miracle, he smiled down at her. And immediately regretted it. Althaea's face went white, and she stumbled and sank against his chest, her eyes rolling back in her head.

"Good God," he muttered, looking about somewhat frantically and trying to keep her from sliding to the ground. No assistance appeared, and with a curse he bent and scooped her up in his arms to carry her off the dance floor.

"What have you done to my Althaea?" her mother

asked, gasping as she hurried toward them, several other mamas in tow.

"I have done nothing," he snapped, pushing past the mob and carrying the girl to a settee in the anteroom. He carefully set her down and stepped aside to escape back into the ballroom.

Thomas Elder was standing there waiting for him. "Is Althaea all right?" he asked, glancing over Nicholas's shoulder.

He nodded, walking over to the refreshment table for a glass of punch and eyeing the nearest gossips until they moved away. He would have preferred brandy, but there was none available downstairs. "She fainted."

"Fainted?" Thomas asked incredulously. "In the middle of a waltz?"

"Yes," Nicholas said indignantly, "she swooned. I smiled, and she swooned."

Thomas snorted, "You're bamming me."

The herd of mamas emerged from the anteroom to glare at him. "God's blood," he grumbled, what remained of his good humor quickly evaporating. "Do they think I ravished her out on the dance floor?"

"If anyone could, it would be you," Thomas answered. "No, don't scowl at me. Just let me thank you for blackmailing me into dancing with Kate. She's lovely."

"Kate?" Nicholas asked, distracted by the sight of Althaea cautiously returning to one of the chairs in the ballroom.

"Miss Ralston," Thomas reminded him, following his gaze. "I'll go see how Althaea is," the viscount offered, patting Nicholas on the shoulder.

"Please do," Nicholas said feelingly. "I'm bloody well not going near her again."

Despite the condition of Miss Hillary, none of the other ladies Nicholas asked to dance refused him and, fortunately, no one else suffered so much as an attack of the vapors. Even so, he was grateful when the music began for the evening's last waltz. Unless he missed his guess, the only thing Miss Ralston would be suffering from was a rather refreshing case of honesty and quick wits. He turned to find her, but she was not in sight. A further perusal also failed to reveal Clarey and the baroness. Cursing under his breath, he again found his mother.

"Have you seen the Hamptons lately, Mama?" he asked coolly, trying to keep his jaw from clenching.

"They left about half an hour ago, Nicky. Kate, I think she had a partner for every dance tonight. She was very tired."

"Damned ungrateful chit," Nicholas muttered, and left the room, unaware of the surprised look on his mother's face as he turned his back.

Katherine wasn't surprised when Lady Alison suggested they leave the ball early. It was true that she was tired, and that her head was beginning to throb with all of the introductions and subsequent invitations and plans, but she had a suspicion it was more than just her health that concerned her godmother. She had learned enough about the etiquette of the *haut ton* to know that dancing twice in one evening with the same man, particularly one with the reputation of the Duke of Sommesby, was enough to put a lady's reputation at risk.

That was not to say she hadn't been tempted to stay. Her initial annoyance at his high-handedness had faded as each successive partner had appeared to be introduced. They had all been witty and charming, and for the first time in a long while she had begun feel like the fair maiden of the tales she had enjoyed as a young girl. It had been a marvelous evening, and to her surprise she had the infamous Black Duke to thank for it.

"I don't know what got into Nick tonight," Lady Alison commented on the tail of her thought. "I've never seen him go out of his way to be charming. Even when Althaea fainted he barely batted an eye."

"Thought he didn't care for those schoolroom misses,"

Neville added, then smiled. "He almost seemed respectable. Another of his games, I imagine."

When they arrived back at the town house Katherine stopped and impulsively stood on tiptoe to kiss Lady Alison, and then Lord Neville, on the cheek. "Thank you," she said. "I had a wonderful time."

"You're welcome, Kate. I'm rather enjoying the idea of bringing a daughter out into society." Lady Alison smiled and hugged her. "Go up to bed, now, child."

Katherine did as she was bid, and Emmie helped her change into her nightgown. Once the maid was gone she picked up her dance card again, gazing at the last name. It was wrong to have left without a word. She shrugged. With all the goings-on of the evening, Nicholas Varon undoubtedly would have forgotten her by the morrow. She threw the card into the wastebasket beside her dressing table and climbed into bed. Ten minutes later she rose again, retrieved it, and placed it in the top drawer of her dresser.

5

"**N**ick, good morning," Clarey greeted Sommesby as he entered the Hamptons' library sharply at ten. The baron crossed the room to shake his hand and motioned him to one of the overstuffed chairs that sat before the fire. Clarey shut the door behind them, a precaution Nicholas noted with some interest.

"Tea? Or perhaps brandy?"

Nicholas seated himself. "It's a bit early for brandy, even for me," he muttered. "Tea will be fine."

Neville poured it, leaning over to hand Nicholas's to him. For a long moment he stared at the fire. "I need to ask you a favor," he said finally.

"I'm listening." He hadn't heard that Clarey was in financial difficulties, but the Hamptons were good friends to his mother, and if they needed funds he would do what he could.

"There is a piece of property several days north of here that I believe is going to come onto the market very soon, and very quietly. I cannot be involved with it myself, nor will I name the present owner to you, but I would like you to purchase it, however shady the deal appears to be. I want the deed, and assurances from the current . . . occupant that it is the property, the manor, and everything in it, including the crop and the contents of the stables, that you are purchasing. And I want the occupant off the property as soon as possible."

The request wasn't remotely what Nicholas had expected, and he gave a low whistle. "You don't ask much, do you?"

Neville nodded. "And one more thing. I want no one to know of this. Besides you, only Alice and I know of this conversation. And Nick, no other questions asked." He took a breath. "Will you help me?"

Greatly intrigued, the duke leaned forward. "I do have one question."

"Yes?"

"What's the name of the property?"

"Crestley Hall."

It appeared that the Season wouldn't be as dull as he had originally thought. "All right." He sat back again and took a sip of tea.

Neville slapped the arm of his chair. "Thank you."

"You're welcome." Nicholas set the cup and saucer aside. "I'd best be on my way, then. It seems my man and I have a great deal of work to do."

"There is one more thing." Neville grimaced. "You may not like this. Of course all of your expenses shall be repaid, but depending on a separate set of circumstances, it may not be for two years."

The conditions were odd, but no more than was the rest of the deal. He shook his head. "You needn't worry, Neville. I could purchase all the homes along Rotten Row and still have enough to buy a lady's heart."

Clarey laughed. "There's not enough money in all the world for that."

"I wonder." He leaned forward. "I am curious about one thing. Why me?"

The baron cleared his throat. "I believed I could trust you, and that you would have the means, and . . ." He trailed off.

"And the necessary lack of scruples?" Nicholas supplied, more intrigued than annoyed. Crestley Hall was sounding more interesting every moment.

Neville had the good manners to look embarrassed. "Something like that."

A soft knock came at the door, and it swung open. "Lord Neville?"

Both men rose at the sound of the female voice. Katherine Ralston stood in the doorway, looking very fetching in a mauve riding outfit cut in the military style. On her head, tilted forward at a jaunty angle, perched a hat of the same color. She looked startled as she saw the duke, but quickly recovered herself.

"I'm sorry, I didn't realize you had company," she said to her godfather. "Lady Alison asked me to tell you that a crate just arrived from Paris. She said you would want to know."

Neville grinned and rubbed his hands together. "Oh, yes. I tracked down a case of some of the finest French wine I've yet encountered, and finally last month convinced the man to sell it to me. This must be it. Thank you, m'dear." He headed for the door, then looked back. "Will you excuse me for a moment?"

Nicholas grinned. "You and your wines. Of course. Miss Ralston and I will endeavor to entertain ourselves." He glanced over in time to see her blush.

Clarey hurried from the room, distracted enough that he voluntarily left his goddaughter alone in the company of the Black Duke. From the warmth in the baron's voice when he spoke to her, Miss Ralston was more than merely tolerated at Hampton House, Nicholas noted with some interest. She continued to stand there looking nervous, and he decided that it served her right.

"I was surprised to see you here," she said finally.

"You left early last night," he responded, leaning against the edge of the end table and crossing his arms.

"I had a headache," she countered.

He looked her carefully up and down, noting that she blushed again. "You seem to have recovered."

"Yes, thank you." She turned, and he thought she was going to flee. Instead she became absorbed in studying the titles of the books on the nearest shelf.

"You like Shakespeare?" he asked, stepping closer. She was smaller than he remembered. Perhaps it was her temper that had made her seem taller.

"I beg your pardon?" she asked over her shoulder.

"Shakespeare," he repeated, reaching over her shoulder for a volume. As he had expected, she started.

"Yes," she mumbled. "I do, very much," she continued after a moment, and stepped around him.

"My mother has a fabulous collection of early quartos," he continued, putting the book back and turning to keep her in sight. "I'm certain she would be delighted to show them off to you."

"Thank you for telling me." She turned to look at him. "And thank you for your assistance last night. I very much enjoyed meeting all of my partners."

"You're welcome," he answered, and leaned against the bookshelf. "Would it have been so terrible for you to have danced again with *me?*" he murmured, wondering what pretty lie her excuse would be.

She looked him in the eye. "I didn't want a scandal."

"The devil, you say!" he retorted. "Do you think I would have danced with all of those weak-kneed, simpering chits, if not to avoid a scandal?" She continued to glare at him, though he had no idea why. "I told you, you did me a good turn. I don't ruin people who do me favors, intentional or not."

"How gracious of you," she responded ungraciously. "I shan't mistake your chivalrous motivations next time."

He straightened. "Who's to say you'll have the chance?"

She put a hand to her forehead as though in distress, uncomfortably reminding him of Althaea Hillary. Her words, though, were anything but those of a demure young miss. "Oh, please, don't say you'll never waltz with me again. I couldn't survive the deprivation!"

Truly irritated now, he took a step forward. She must have seen something in his face, for her hand lowered and she stepped backward. "Waltzing again with me should be the least of your worries, Miss Ralston," he said with a growl. "I think there are other social graces you have more need to perfect."

"What? How dare you, of all people, lecture me on proper behavior?" she hissed, her eyes flashing.

She had a point, but he was angry enough that he didn't care. "It's obvious that someone needs to," he returned, taking another step closer and noting her fast breathing and the flush on her cheeks. Apparently she wasn't quite as composed as she wanted him to believe.

She backed away again. "You, sir," she spat out, "are a great beast."

"I've been called worse," he murmured, tempted to take the pretty chit over his knee.

"And with good reason, I'm certain," she retorted, and ducked sideways to put the couch between them. "Now, if you will excuse me, I have a far more pleasant diversion to prepare for."

Not finished venting his anger, and at any rate unwilling to let her have the last word, Nicholas pursued her to the doorway and blocked her exit with his body. "And what might that be?"

She stopped in front of him and put her hands on her hips. "Not that it's any of your concern, but I am going picnicking with some of the parties you were so kind as to provide me introduction to last evening."

"You're—" he began, and then changed his mind. It appeared that she wasn't aware of the identities of all the guests invited to the al fresco luncheon.

"Yes," she went on scathingly, "and *they* apparently have found no fault with my manners."

"You little hoyden," he snapped. "You won't be picnicking with anyone after I ask them to beg off." Nicholas turned and headed through the doorway.

She gasped. "You wouldn't."

It wasn't her words that stopped him, but her tone of voice. He turned to see that she was shaking, her face white. Something abruptly made him wonder how long she had been alone before her arrival at Hampton House. Perhaps he wasn't the only one whose list of acquaintances was far longer than that of friends. "No," he said slowly, "I wouldn't." He cleared his throat. "Good day, Miss Ralston."

With that he was out the door. He collected his hat and greatcoat and left without a word to Neville, wondering, of all things, how anyone's eyes could be so blue.

6

By the time the Viscount of Sheresford arrived to escort her to Hyde Park, Kate had begun to calm down. What nerve Nicholas Varon had, to threaten never to dance with her again, for heaven's sake, even after she had thanked him for his help. She knew she had a temper herself, but no one had ever looked at her that way before, and it had frightened her a little.

There was nothing frightening in the Viscount of Sheresford's gaze as she met him in the hall. "By heaven," he exclaimed, looking at her admiringly, "if you ain't slap up to the echo."

It was exactly what she needed to put her in good humor again. She laughed and curtseyed. "Thank you, milord."

He hurried forward to pull her upright. "Thomas, please," he said.

She smiled. "Thank you, Thomas."

By the time they reached Hyde Park they were a party of five, having been joined by Captain Reg Hillary, his younger sister Althaea, apparently recovered from her fainting spell, and Sir John Dremond's daughter, Louisa. Lord Neville had given Kate a spirited gray mare named Winter, and when Thomas suggested they head off the main drag to the more open area of the park, she readily agreed.

"What are you looking for?" the viscount asked a few moments later, following her gaze toward a group of riders a hundred yards distant.

She hadn't realized she was being so obvious. "I was just wondering if the Duke of Sommesby rode here." She wasn't precisely looking for him, except to be certain that he wasn't near, the blackguard.

"Nick? He does, though he usually likes to come earlier, when it's less crowded. I thought I'd finally talked him into coming with us today, but his groom met me at my gate with a note begging off. Said that something had come up."

Katherine flushed. That explained why their party wasn't an even number. She knew very well what the something had been, and wondered why he hadn't mentioned that he was to be a member of their group when they had argued. "I'm certain it was important."

Thomas snorted. "With Nick there's no telling what it was."

Althaea and the captain had brought hampers with them, and they settled for their picnic in the shade of an old oak. Katherine peeled a peach and laughed as Reg told a story about how he and his six brothers and sisters had convinced three governesses in succession that their house was haunted.

"A skill for strategy you put to good use against bonny Bonaparte," Thomas noted, raising his glass of Madeira.

"At least someone in the family has courage," Althaea said ruefully, and her brother reached over and patted her hand.

An argument about the stallion that Thomas had just purchased, at an apparently outrageous price, followed, and the two men rose to examine the bay.

"Althaea, what in the world happened last night?" Louisa Dremond asked in a whisper when the three women were alone.

"Oh, I was so embarrassed," the girl muttered, blushing. "Mama is convinced that the Black Duke is ready to settle, and that I'm the one who can bring him to his senses. I just don't want to marry anyone who's so ... fierce. It would be simply awful if he were to offer for me."

Kate agreed. To be married to such an odious, high-handed villain would be nearly as bad as handing Crestley Hall over to Uncle Simon. Thomas and the captain returned, and as they loaded the hampers Louisa took Katherine aside.

"I don't know if you remember," the slim, merry blond said quietly, "but you and I came out in the same Season. I was sorry to hear about your father."

"Thank you," Katherine replied, touched.

"When you left London, my mama had been about to invite you and your mother over for tea. I would like to extend that invitation now to you and the baroness, if you would care to come."

Impulsively Katherine took the girl's hand. "Thank you again. I will speak to Lady Alison, but I'm certain she will be delighted."

Katherine returned to Hampton House in high spirits, and informed Lady Alison of their invitation. "It's good to see color in your cheeks again," her godmother said with a smile. "You were such a sprite when you were younger, and I had begun to fear that your uncle had driven it out of you."

Kate tossed her head. "I wouldn't let him," she answered defiantly.

Her godmother chuckled. "I'm so pleased you're making friends. I never thought I'd say it, but Nick was a godsend last night." She straightened. "Which reminds me. Something arrived for you." She led the way into the drawing room.

Kate thought that it would be some of her things from Crestley, but instead, in the middle of the table at the end of the low couch, between a Chinese jade dragon and a wooden African elephant carving, perched a tall vase full of white roses. In the center of the fragrant mass a single red rose stood out like a drop of blood. A card leaned against the narrow base of the fine crystal.

With a deep breath she picked up the envelope. Her name was written across the cream-colored parchment in a bold hand that she already had come to recognize. Her heart began to beat faster as she pulled out the card, though she couldn't say why that was so. The writing inside was equally familiar. All it said was "Apologies." It was signed, "Varon."

When, at luncheon two days later, Louisa and her mother, Lady Mary, discovered that the closest Kate had ever been to the opera was a Christmas pageant at the All Souls Church back home in Staffordshire, they immediately invited her and Lady Alison to join them in their box that evening. More of Katherine's dresses had arrived, and with Emmie's help she donned a low-cut gold silk creation with short, puffy sleeves and full, looped skirts. Her maid pulled her hair up and curled the long ends to let them hang in black spirals down her back. Lady Alison knocked and came in as Emmie was finishing Katherine's tresses.

"This is too much, I think," Kate muttered, eyeing herself critically.

"Nonsense," Lady Alison chided her, then smiled. "Though I doubt that any gentlemen present tonight will be watching *The Marriage of Figaro.*" She chuckled. "More likely they'll be daydreaming of their own blissful nuptials."

"Lady Alison!" Kate exclaimed, blushing, then laughed. "Oh, dear."

The Dremonds' coach brought them to the opera house, and while the older women stopped in the lobby to greet friends, Louisa took Kate by the arm and led her up the narrow stairs to the row of boxes on the left side of the stage. "The best part of going to the opera," Louisa said, pushing through a set of curtains, "is watching everyone watching everyone else."

Kate chuckled. "What about the music and the singing?"

"Oh, posh on that."

Abruptly Louisa stopped, tugging Kate back against the wall. A slim blond woman walked toward them along the narrow hallway behind the boxes. Her red gown was even more low-cut than Kate's, and a matching tall red plume waved above her hair. The woman passed by them without even glancing over, and headed for the stairs. Directly behind her sauntered the Duke of Sommesby, a dark vision in black and gray. He stopped as he saw her, then nodded.

"Good evening, Miss Ralston," he intoned. "Miss Dremond."

Louisa curtsied. "Your Grace."

"You enjoy opera?" he queried, his eyes swiftly taking in Katherine from head to toe and back again.

"I don't know," she answered, lifting her chin and refusing to blush at his scrutiny. "I've never been before."

"Nicky," came a simpering voice from behind her, "come downstairs, darling."

"In a moment, Eloise," he answered, flicking a glance at the woman, just the faintest touch of annoyance in his gray eyes. "You've made a good choice for your first opera, then," he continued, his gaze returning to Katherine. "Mozart seems able to provide something for every taste." He smiled.

"I'll wait for you in the lobby, dear. Don't be long talking to these children."

Annoyed at the insult, Katherine cleared her throat as the woman departed. "Apparently Mozart failed in her case," she muttered to Louisa, who giggled.

The duke had moved past Louisa to follow the woman, and he stopped in mid-stride, his sharp look setting Katherine back a little. He leaned forward, blocking her from Louisa. "Miss LeMonde's interests need be no concern of yours, Miss Ralston," he returned.

More annoyed now, Katherine glanced away to see that Miss LeMonde was no longer in sight. "Apparently your interests are no concern of hers," she replied, "as you seem to want to stay."

The duke straightened. "Eloise's interests are whatever I wish them to be," he murmured, and turned on his heel to follow the woman.

"How unfortunate for you," Kate replied in an equally soft voice, refusing to blush even though she could guess what he was implying.

His back stiffened, but the duke ignored her comment otherwise and continued on his way. In a moment he was gone, through the curtains and down the steps. Kate turned to find Louisa staring at her.

"Weren't you afraid of him?" her friend muttered, pulling her forward to their box.

"The Duke of Sommesby?" Kate replied. "Never." She glanced back to make certain that Lady Alison and Lady Mary hadn't arrived yet. "That woman with him, was she the one who almost caused that duel before?"

Louisa shook her head and leaned closer. "No. That was Josette Bettreaux. The duke sent her off to Paris. You would definitely know her if you saw her. She's . . . stunning. I don't know who Eloise LeMonde is. She must be a new one." She sighed. "She is beautiful, though."

Kate tilted her head and looked out over the audience below to find that, as Lady Alison had predicted, several pairs of opera glasses were turned in her direction. "I don't think he likes her very much," she replied.

Louisa blushed. "I don't suppose that matters," she whispered, then giggled.

Kate smiled back, though surprisingly she didn't feel much amused. "I suppose not." She wondered how the Black Duke felt about Josette Bettreaux, and if he would ask her to come back from Paris.

As the other ladies arrived, Louisa pointed out who held the other boxes around the theater. The one that lay two sections closer to the stage than the Dremonds' box was the Duke of Sommesby's. Katherine glanced over at it several times during the evening. It remained empty.

* * *

The Berresford ball was rumored to be the grandest assembly of the Season, and Louisa and Althaea had talked of little else for a week. Everyone was supposed to be there, and Kate wondered if that was true.

"Miss Kate?"

Katherine started and looked into the mirror to see Emmie's reflection gazing back at her. "Yes, Emmie?"

"You're finished, milady," the maid said, her tone making it clear that this was not the first time she had spoken.

"Thank you," Katherine said, rising. "I must have been daydreaming."

Smiling, she walked over to the full-length mirror and twirled around. Emmie had somehow managed to pull her hair up, arranging the tendrils that insisted on escaping into a soft frame around her face and neck. Her deep-rose silk gown with lighter-colored lace at her neck and frothing at the end of her half sleeves had rose beads sewn throughout the body, and she shimmered with every movement. It wasn't as simple as she liked, but she had to admit that the effect was pleasing.

Thomas's opinion was less restrained as the viscount met her and the Hamptons at the side of the ballroom. "You are a goddess, Kate," he breathed, and bowed low over her hand, his sandy hair falling into his eyes.

She chuckled. "Thank you, Thomas."

"It looks to be a sad crush," he noted happily as he led her over to where the rest of their group had already gathered. They exchanged greetings, and then the Viscount abruptly frowned.

"What is it?" she murmured.

"Trouble, no doubt." Thomas grimaced, and Katherine turned to see Francis DuPres approaching. He was obviously still out of sorts over the events of the Albey ball, for though she had caught him looking at her several times over the past days, he hadn't yet approached. Until then.

DuPres reached them, his eyes on her as he bowed.

"Miss Ralston, will you do me the honor of dancing with me this evening?"

Thomas shifted, and she knew that he was about to give DuPres a setdown. The dandy glanced at her companions, and she abruptly wondered if being accepted might be as important to him as it had been to her. "Yes, Mr. DuPres," she answered before Thomas could intervene, and held out her card and pencil so that he could choose the dance himself.

A look she couldn't read briefly crossed his face and then was gone. He almost snatched the card out of her hand in his eagerness to have it. When he had written his name in, he gave it back to her and bowed again. "Until then, Miss Ralston," he said, and walked away.

"Whatever were you thinking?" Thomas asked as she looked down at her card. He had chosen a waltz late in the evening.

"Heavens, everyone's been ignoring him for a week. And perhaps I'll step on his toes, and he'll never ask me again," Kate answered, flashing him a smile.

"More likely *he'll* be stepping on *your* toes," Reg suggested. The orchestra struck up a country dance, and he took Louisa's hand, while Thomas led Katherine out onto the floor and Althaea's partner stepped up to collect her.

The viscount was right; it was a sad crush, and Katherine had never had such a wonderful time. She loved to dance, and did not lack for eager partners. As the evening progressed, though, it became increasingly warm and stuffy in the huge room, and her feet in their thin rose slippers began to ache.

"I believe this is my dance?" a voice said right in her ear, and she jumped.

Francis DuPres held out his hand, and with an apology to Lady Alison she stepped away from the chairs bordering the room and walked out onto the floor. He was only a tolerable dancer, and Reg's comment about whose toes would be stepped on came to mind. When halfway through the waltz he suggested they step out onto the balcony to get some air, Kate thankfully accepted. The night was dark and shadowy after the brightly lit ballroom, and it was blessedly cool. She breathed deeply and sighed, brushing her fingers over the petals of the summer bouquet that filled the blue vase beside her. A dozen more evenly spaced vases covered the length of the stonework railing.

"You are lovely, Kate," DuPres murmured from her side, and he reached over to finger the frothy material at her wrist before he slid his hand down over hers, where it rested on the balcony.

She removed it quickly. "Thank you, Mr. DuPres," she said stiffly, abruptly realizing that she should not have left the room with him.

"Francis," he corrected, moving over smoothly to block her path as she retreated. "Don't go; we haven't had a chance to become acquainted."

They were already acquainted better than she would have liked. "Excuse me," she grated, and started to walk around him.

He grabbed her hand and pulled her up against him. "Come now, Kate, you should be more friendly," he murmured, leaning closer.

She shoved at him, but he was stronger than she. "Let go," she commanded, angry.

"Not until I claim my prize," he insisted, and yanked her closer still.

His other hand reached up to grab the back of her neck and pull her head forward. His lips touched her cheek, seeking her mouth. Very angry and very frightened, Kate shut her eyes and at the same time lifted her knee. Hard.

An explosion of hot breath blasted her face as DuPres doubled over. Before he could straighten again, something yanked him backward onto the hard stone. A figure clothed all in black hauled DuPres back to his feet, and then dragged him over to where Katherine stood.

"Apologize to Miss Ralston," came the quiet voice of Nicholas Varon. Even in the dim light it was clear that the Black Duke was furious.

"I'll kill you for this, Sommesby," DuPres wheezed, still half doubled over.

The duke shook him by the collar and shoved him away. "Apologize, or you can try it at dawn with pistols," Nicholas said, even more quietly than before.

Nicholas Varon was not the only one who was angry. Now that she had gotten over the initial shock of the assault, Kate was furious. This was her battle, and she didn't need the Black Duke to fight it for her. As DuPres faced Sommesby, she stepped sideways, grabbed one of the pretty blue vases, and raised it over her head. "Don't touch me again, you cad," she said with a growl, and dashed the vase against the side of his head. It shattered, water and flowers and pieces of porcelain going everywhere, and with a grunt Francis DuPres collapsed among the debris.

Sommesby took a step backward, his eyes on DuPres. After a moment he looked up at her, his expression one of stunned surprise, then glanced down and flicked a piece of daisy off his lapel. When he raised his head again, his eyes were dancing. "Well done, Miss Ralston," he murmured.

Breathing hard, Kate unclenched her hands and sagged back against the railing. DuPres remained slumped on the stone where he had fallen. "Oh, my," she whispered, beginning to realize exactly what she had done.

The duke stepped over the mess to steady her with both hands on her shoulders. "Are you all right?"

"I'm trying to decide if I'm going to faint."

He chuckled and pulled her closer. "I somehow don't think you're the fainting type," he noted.

She wound her trembling hands into his jacket and rested her cheek on his shoulder while he held her. Perhaps he wasn't as dastardly as she had thought. Laughter sounded from inside the doorway, and she started and pulled away. He released her immediately, but putting distance between them left her little reassured. To be out here on the balcony with a man—or, worse, two men—was enough to ruin her. If anyone found out that she had knocked one of them unconscious, her godparents would probably have to ship her off to America and she'd never see Crestley again. "Your Grace, please don't tell," she begged, paling, and regretting every cutting remark she had made to him over the past weeks.

"No worries," the duke replied immediately, his expression still amused. "This is a secret I shall very much enjoy keeping." He glanced back at DuPres. "And if our sleeping fool has any pride at all, I don't believe he'll be repeating the tale, either." His eyes met hers and slid to the doorway. "I do believe we should exit the battleground before we are discovered, however."

She nodded, then glanced into the gloom of the balcony behind him. "You are out here alone?" she whispered.

He gazed at her for a moment, then nodded. "You refer, of course, to Eloise LeMonde."

Katherine shrugged, reluctant to anger him. "I wasn't—"

"Her interests, if she has any, are her own," he replied, and pursed his lips ruefully. "How was *Figaro?*"

She smiled. "Wonderful," she replied enthusiastically. Impulsively she touched his sleeve. "Thank you again for helping me, Your Grace," she said, looking up at him.

"You're welcome, Miss Ralston," he answered.

"Kate," she said.

"Beg pardon?" he queried, raising an eyebrow.

"Please call me Kate," she explained. They were conspirators of a sort now, and she owed him for keeping her secret.

He looked down at her for a long moment, then shook his head. "Katherine suits you better," he said thoughtfully.

DuPres groaned, and Sommesby took her hand and tucked it over his arm. "You shouldn't be here when he emerges. I think you should have another headache." His lips quirked. "You won't be the only one with a pounding skull tonight, I'll wager."

She nodded, smiling uncertainly at him. He wasn't exactly whom she would have imagined as a chivalrous ally, but something in his eyes as he looked down at her made Katherine believe that he would keep his word. "Thank you again."

Just inside the ballroom he looked sideways at her. "By the way, my friends call me Nick," he murmured.

Katherine took a breath, wondering what she was about to get herself into. "Then I shall call you Nicholas," she returned, and was rewarded by a surprised look that quickly turned to one of appreciation and then was as swiftly gone.

He started forward again and nodded. "Nicholas it is, then."

7

Fhrom a distance Nicholas watched Katherine explain to her godparents what had happened. Neville's already ruddy face went redder as the two women were forced to head him away from the balcony. After a moment of hushed argument they left the room. When they were well away Nicholas made his way over to where his mother sat with Lady Ann Sefton.

"Mama," he drawled, "I believe it is time for us to depart."

She looked up at him curiously, but when he said nothing else she took leave of her companion and accepted the arm he offered her. "What is going on?" she murmured.

"Something rather interesting just happened, and I don't want you to pay for it," he returned, nodding as they passed the Hillarys.

"Oh, dear." She sighed. "What this time?"

"Francis DuPres is, how shall I say, sleeping, out on the balcony. I imagine he'll be coming around any moment now," he said mildly, and her fingers tightened around his sleeve.

"Mon dieu, what happened?"

"He was pawing Katherine Ralston." As he remembered her frightened face he had to fight the temptation to return to the balcony and throw Francis DuPres off of it. "Quite vulgar of him, actually. He should have realized a true rake would never stoop to such methods for a kiss," he said, trying to make light of the incident. "Charming a lady out of her favors is a much more satisfying task."

"Nicholas," his mother reproved with a reluctant smile. "Kate is all right?"

"She's fine." He grinned as he signaled for her shawl and his greatcoat to be brought to them. "In fact, she did a rather excellent job of rescuing herself. I felt quite unneeded."

"Oh, yes?" Julia Varon queried, eyeing him closely.

He recognized the look. "Don't get any ideas, Mama. She's barely out of the schoolroom, for God's sake."

"You're hardly in your dotage, Nicky," his mother replied with a smile. "She stands up to you, yes?"

"She's hardheaded," he retorted, looking away from the amused curiosity on her face and hoping she wouldn't set Kate Ralston dangling after him. He wanted nothing to do with any schoolroom chits or their missish prattle. In all honesty, though, he couldn't picture Miss Ralston setting her cap at anyone. And woe to the man who attempted to obtain her favors without her permission.

To his relief Julia dropped the subject, and he saw her to her coach with no more than a few commonplace exchanges about the weather and upcoming social events. When she was gone he signaled for his own coach and headed off to one of his clubs, though his thoughts turned often enough to an outspoken schoolroom chit armed with a vase of flowers that he lost a hundred and fifty pounds at hazard.

The next morning his man of business met him in his study with news about the status of Crestley Hall. "Well, Gladstone, what have we gotten ourselves into?" he asked with a smile.

"A great deal of trouble, if you ask me, Your Grace," Gladstone returned, fingering his graying moustache.

"Details, please," he returned. "And you remembered my instructions?"

"Yes, Your Grace, though I have told you that I do not like to work under these conditions. It is folly for you to invest any of your money in something that you seem determined to know so little about."

"And?" Nicholas prompted after a moment.

Gladstone shifted some papers about the desk. "The owner's representative is calling himself Jonathan Smith."

Nicholas smiled at the distaste in Gladstone's voice. "I told you what kind of purchase this was likely to be."

"Yes, Your Grace. I did not expect the man to be so obvious about it, however." He paused, and Nicholas could practically see the wheels turning in the older man's head. "The story is that a youth has inherited the property but will not actually come into possession of it for another two years. This young man does not wish to keep Crestley Hall, but would be willing to entertain a cash offer for it."

"So the problem is only that the boy is too young to inherit," Nicholas commented, disbelieving that to be the difficulty.

Apparently Gladstone did as well. "I doubt it, Your Grace. Mr. Smith went to great lengths to keep the young man's name from me. It is more likely being sold out from under the boy."

"So," Nicholas muttered darkly, briefly wondering how the Baron of Clarey had become involved in these shady dealings and what, exactly, the attraction of Crestley Hall might be. Gladstone opened his mouth, but Nicholas raised a hand. "And you are about to tell me that you could easily get to the bottom of all of this."

"Yes, Your Grace."

"Don't," Varon said shortly. He was damned curious himself, but Neville's instructions had been quite explicit, and he would honor them. To a point.

"Well, you will be forced to find out eventually," Gladstone said morosely. "The boy must sign the deed. If the names are false, the paper is worthless. At this point I'm not convinced that the document would be legal, anyway."

Nicholas leaned forward. "You make certain it is legal,

Gladstone. When that deed comes into my hand, I want no one in England to be able to contest it. Understand?"

"Your Grace, that may be close to impossible."

"That's what I pay you for, isn't it?"

Gladstone sighed. "Yes, Your Grace."

"It's a shame you left the Berresfords' early," Thomas commented several hours later as the viscount rode beside him to Richmond Park.

"Oh," Nicholas asked innocently, "why is that?"

"Someone put a vase across Francis DuPres's skull."

"Really? Whatever for?" Innocence was something he was bad at, Nicholas was finding, for he hadn't had much practice. Under any other circumstances he wouldn't have given a second thought about claiming responsibility for the deed himself. But Kate Ralston was right. There would be a scandal, and while he had little to fear, she might be ruined. That hardly seemed fair, when all she had done was show more spirit than any woman he had ever met. He would keep her secret.

"He didn't say," Thomas answered slowly, looking at him closely. "In fact, he claimed that he stumbled in the dark and pulled the vase onto his own head."

Nicholas was surprised that DuPres hadn't arisen demanding satisfaction. "Well, he's not the most graceful man I've ever encountered," he drawled. "Perhaps he was telling the truth."

"Yes, perhaps he was," Thomas agreed. The younger man fiddled with his reins for a moment. "I did think it interesting, though, that DuPres and Kate went out onto the balcony, and then you and she reemerged from there several moments later and left." He spoke to his bay's neck, but stiffened when Nicholas glanced over at him sharply.

"Oh, you did, did you?" he muttered.

"Yes."

"If you saw him and Miss Ralston leave the ballroom, then why didn't you go after her?" he asked shortly. "You're the one who warned me about DuPres."

"I was on my way over when you came back inside," Thomas answered, looking hurt.

"You never should have let him near her in the first place," Nicholas went on, refusing to be appeased.

"I could say the same about you," Thomas retorted, red-faced.

Nicholas sneered. "Jealous, are we? Don't worry, Thomas. She's too innocent for me."

Thomas flushed. "She asks about you, you know," he said abruptly, and kicked his horse into a canter as they reached the boundary of the park. "You're hard to compete with when you're not even around to show her your bad side," he said over his shoulder.

Nicholas couldn't stop the amused smile that quirked his lips for a moment as he kneed his own coal black stallion and caught up to the viscount. So she asked about him, did she? Perhaps she wasn't as immune to his charms as she apparently wanted him to think. "I see you didn't take my advice about that nag," he noted, attempting to change the subject. "What's his name, Orchid?"

"Orpheus," Thomas corrected hotly. "And I'd pit him against your bad-tempered brute any time."

"Orpheus against Ulysses? An epic battle indeed," Varon commented dryly.

Thomas snorted, then grinned reluctantly. "Odious fellow," he muttered. "Fifty pounds says my hero can beat yours. To Darby Bridge, say."

The small wooden bridge was approximately a mile and a half distance across the park, and Nicholas nodded. "Call it," he said, drawing in the reins.

"Now!" Thomas shouted without warning, and was off like a shot.

Undaunted, the duke kicked the black in the ribs. The powerful muscles tensed beneath him as the horse surged forward. He leaned over the sleek neck and gave the animal its head. Three-quarters of the way to the bridge they had caught the bay. By the time they reached the creek Nicholas was a length ahead.

The black wanted to keep going, but he drew it in and circled around to face the panting viscount. "Fifty pounds, Thomas," he said. "How much did you pay for that thing, anyway?"

"Oh, shut up, Nick," Thomas snapped. "One of these days you are going to lose, you know."

"Perhaps," Nicholas replied, amused. "But not today."

8

Uncle Simon didn't write back. Kate hadn't really expected that he would, but foolish as it was, she couldn't help but hope. She considered returning home, but even being at Crestley would do little to keep it safe from him. Instead she made an appointment with Lord Neville's solicitor and asked him to look into the matter.

Mr. Hodges had looked at her askance when she walked into his offices, but once she had explained who she was and that she would be able to pay him for his troubles, he agreed to send someone to see if any paper work had been filed in Staffordshire. It took most of the money she had been able to bring with her, but as the Hamptons insisted that she was part of the family and had been paying all of her bills, she was willing to make the expenditure. If she could hold on to Crestley for two more years, she would need to rely on no one for anything.

Two days after the Berresford ball the Dowager Duchess of Sommesby sent an invitation for Lady Alison and Kate to come for afternoon tea. Though she gladly accepted, the invitation made Kate a bit nervous. If Lady Julia should ask questions about the incident at the ball, she would feel compelled to answer them, and she didn't want to. She still wasn't certain what had possessed her to go out onto the secluded balcony with anyone, much less

Francis DuPres, and would have preferred to forget the entire incident.

When they reached the courtyard of the duchess's magnificent town house, the sight of a beautiful high-perch racing phaeton in the drive increased Kate's anxiety. "Do you think she has other visitors?" she asked Lady Alison as they were handed out of the Hampton carriage by the footman.

"Julia said it was to be just us. We haven't had a chance to talk lately, and she told me she wanted a good coze."

"Are you certain you want me along, then?" Katherine asked, half-hoping her godmother would send her back to Hampton House.

Lady Alison took her hand and squeezed it. "Nonsense. Julia wouldn't have invited you if she didn't want you to come. You know that, child."

"Yes, Lady Alison," she answered dutifully, not much reassured.

When they were led into the drawing room, there was indeed no one there but Lady Julia, and Kate relaxed a little. If there were going to be questions, at least there would be no one else to overhear. To her surprise, though, the Dowager Duchess said nothing about what had transpired at the ball. Instead they spent a delightful time discussing everything from Paris fashions to literature.

"I heard that you have an impressive collection of Shakespeare quartos," Kate said, holding up a tray of tea cakes for Lady Alison.

"Yes. My son has been trying to buy, borrow, or steal them away from me for years. But I have resisted all of his offers. It is the one way I can be assured that he will come to visit me." She smiled and motioned toward the door. "They are in the library, if you wish to see them."

"Are you certain?" Katherine asked, rising.

"*Mais oui.* We mature women have things to discuss, anyway. You will find the library two doors down on the left."

"Thank you, Your Grace."

The library door was closed, but she pushed it open and stepped inside. The first thing that caught her eye was a pair of gleaming black calf-length Hessian boots crossed at the ankles and stretched out in front of one of the chairs by the window. Curious, she stepped quietly forward to see the Duke of Sommesby, an open book propped against his chest and a glass of brandy in his free hand.

He was reading, and she studied his profile. The Black Duke looked relaxed, and judging from the curve of his lips he was enjoying whatever it was that he was reading. He was dressed in blue and gray, his cravat elegant yet simple, in a style she much admired and that she had frequently seen followers of the Black Duke affect.

Without warning he turned his head and looked up at her, and she saw surprise and pleasure in his eyes, quickly blanketed. "Katherine," he said, setting aside the book and coming to his feet.

"I didn't mean to disturb you," she said, taking a step back to look up at him. "Your mother invited Lady Alison and me over for tea," she explained, abruptly feeling as though she had to justify her presence in his mother's library.

"Oh, she did, did she?" he muttered so quietly that she barely caught the words.

"I remembered what you had said about the quartos. She said I might come and look at them," Katherine went on defiantly.

"You do like Shakespeare," he commented, setting the brandy snifter down as well.

"Did you think I was lying?" she asked indignantly. Teddy, the vicar's son back at Crestley, had called her a bluestocking on more than one occasion because of her fondness for the bard, but the duke did not seem overly concerned with the conventions of polite society.

He raised a hand. "I would not accuse a woman with eyes as blue as yours of lying," he said softly.

"Which is to say that if my eyes were brown you would think me a liar?" she asked innocently.

His laughter surprised her. He had a merry laugh and an attractive smile, and the green highlights in his eyes twinkled as he gazed at her. "I won't apologize for the compliment," he said after a moment, turning half away, "but I concede the point."

She hadn't expected him to give in, and was disappointed that he had done so. "Quitter," she muttered, and he froze and turned back to her.

"Beg pardon?" he returned, raising an eyebrow.

"I said you were a quitter," she repeated, quite embarrassed that he had heard her. She would have to remember to mutter more quietly in his presence.

"Do you, perchance, speak to the Viscount of Sheresford and your other male acquaintances in the same flattering manner with which you have honored me?" he queried, not looking offended at all.

"No."

He nodded, pursing his lips. "I thought not." She expected more, but instead he walked over to the near corner of the library and motioned her to follow him. "How goes the conspiracy?" he queried over his shoulder.

"No one seems to know," she answered, and cocked her head at him. "You didn't speak to Lady Julia about it."

He stopped and turned around. "Of course not. She knows merely that DuPres had a slight . . . accident." With a grin he turned away. "Has he bothered you?"

She shook her head. "I've not even seen him."

"Good. You let me know if he approaches you."

Kate stopped and put her hands on her hips. "Are you my protector now, Your Grace?" she queried. "Because I assure you, I don't need one."

The Black Duke leaned against the shelf behind him. "What do you need, Katherine?" he asked quietly, folding his arms over his chest.

The serious look in his eyes surprised her. It was on the tip of her tongue to say, "Crestley Hall," but then he would think that she was a helpless female in need of rescuing. "What everyone needs, I suppose," she answered.

"Love, friendship, laughter, kindness." She smiled self-consciously, thinking what a goosecap he must find her. "And chocolate creams."

He laughed again. "I shall remember that," he responded, his eyes merry as he looked at her. "You are an unusual woman." After another moment he pushed himself away from the shelf and swept his arm out. "Here you are," he said, indicating a shelf of old and incredibly fragile-looking paperbound quartos and folios, carefully protected behind glass. He unhooked the latch and swung the glass sideways. "Except for *The Two Gentlemen of Verona*, which I have."

She stepped forward, and he moved back, out of her way. These were indeed early quartos and folios. One of them even looked to be an original playbook, one that William Shakespeare himself might have held.

"Go ahead," he said encouragingly.

She reached her hand out, then lowered it again. "They look so fragile. I'm afraid to touch them."

"Which one?" he asked from right behind her.

"King Lear, I think," she whispered, wondering why the deep, dry sound of his voice made her want to lean back against him.

His hand reached over her shoulder, much as it had when they fought in the Hamptons' library. He pulled down the quarto and handed it to her. As his hand left the manuscript, his fingers brushed her cheek, and she shuddered.

She knew that she should move, walk over to one of the chairs or to the deep windowsill, but instead she stood like a statue, holding the manuscript carefully in her hands and afraid to breathe. His fingers touched her cheek again, brushing the skin so lightly it made her shiver. The other hand touched her shoulder, and she turned around as though under a spell.

"You should never turn your back on a gentleman of ill repute," he chided, his fingers still cupping her cheek. "Even a cowhearted quitter like myself."

She agreed wholeheartedly, but still didn't speak. If she did he might stop looking at her in that way that was making her stomach flutter and her heart beat so fast.

"What, no argument?" he continued in the same quiet voice. "No witty sally for me? Cat got your tongue, Kate?"

Nicholas took a step closer, and with his fingers tilted her face up. The Black Duke leaned down and touched his lips to hers in a faintly brandy-flavored kiss. Katherine's eyes shut at the contact. Shivers ran up and down her spine and into the tips of her fingers and toes, and she leaned into him. His hand slid down from her shoulder to her waist, and he pulled her closer. Something began to slip from her fingers. . . .

"The play!" she cried, her voice muffled against his mouth, and she bent forward, bumping her head, to grab the fragile pages before they could strike the floor. She trapped the quarto against her calf and carefully picked it up again. Only then did she look at Nicholas.

He stood a few feet away, rubbing his chin and glaring at her. "Ouch."

"Well, it was your own fault," she retorted, determined not to let him see how much he had unsettled her.

"I see you've recovered the power of speech," he returned, stepping forward.

She backed away, clutching the quarto to her chest like a shield. "Stay away from me," she warned.

"A little late to be acting shy," he commented, coming closer anyway. "Don't tell me you were displeased."

"Being displeased or not has nothing to do with it," she replied, stopping with her back against a shelf of books. Nicholas Varon was dangerous in a way that she hadn't imagined. She had been schooled for her entire life on how to be a proper lady, but at this moment what she wanted more than anything was for the scoundrel to kiss her again.

"So you did like it," he responded, grinning and pursuing her into the corner.

Her heart pounding, she nearly gave in. "You, sir," she said desperately, "are a rakehell."

He stopped. For a moment he looked at her, then nodded and took a step back. "And you, Katherine, are a lady." He bowed elegantly. "My apologies."

Katherine exhaled.

Abruptly he strode forward and took her shoulders in his hands. "But you were wrong. I am not a quitter," he murmured, running his finger along her lower lip. With that he turned and left the room.

After a dazed moment in which she nearly walked out of the library with *King Lear*, Kate shakily replaced the play behind its protective glass. She returned to the drawing room to see Lady Alison just rising to come and get her.

"Ready to go, Kate?" she asked, smiling.

Katherine cleared her throat. "Yes."

Julia Varon rose as well. "Did I hear Nicky's voice in the hallway?" she asked curiously. "He said he might stop by today."

Katherine nodded. "Yes. He was in the library," she mumbled, knowing that she must be blushing.

The Dowager Duchess nodded thoughtfully. "Ah. He often goes there."

As they took their leave Katherine thought she heard the duchess chuckling, but she couldn't be certain.

9

He shouldn't have kissed her.

It had been a muttonheaded thing to do, something he would have expected of a schoolboy on his first trip to London in search of town bronze. Nicholas berated himself on the entire drive back to his town house, distracted enough that he nearly ran down the Viscountess of Franton before he noticed her yammering French poodles and swerved the team. He hadn't meant to kiss her. He had only meant to tease her, to remind the little madcap that she should not be placing herself in a position where she was alone in a room with a man. But then, as if of its own accord, his hand had touched her cheek, and she had trembled.

He had always sought women who knew the rules of the game, and who, without exception, had played it before. They appreciated his attentions, or so they claimed, and he rewarded them for their time and discretion. And not one of them had ever trembled at his touch. And not one of them would have named laughter or friendship, or chocolate creams, as more necessary than wealth or comfort.

Gladstone was waiting in his study. Nicholas wanted time to think, but Clarey had impressed on him the importance of time in the acquisition of Crestley Hall, so he threw his gloves on the desk and sank into the chair behind it. "Well?"

The older man didn't even blink. "There is a legal precedent in our favor, if the boy and the legal guardian both sign the deed."

"Grand," Nicholas said with a growl, and got to his feet. "If that's all—"

"Not quite, sir." Gladstone glanced up from the stack of papers he held.

Nicholas cursed and seated himself again. "Make it quick, will you?"

"I'm trying, Your Grace."

"Be very careful, Gladstone," Nicholas murmured, leaning back. "I am not in a good mood."

His secretary swallowed. "Yes, Your Grace." He consulted his papers again. "First of all, there are apparently several other parties interested in Crestley, and—"

"Competition?" Nicholas cut in, sitting forward again. "Why?" he muttered, mostly to himself.

"You haven't allowed me to discover that, Your Grace, but I assume that because of the situation and the price, any number of miscreants might be looking at this as a way to buy themselves into society."

"Miscreants?" Varon repeated, raising an eyebrow.

Gladstone flushed. "Not you, of course, Your Grace."

Nicholas waved a hand at him. "Outbid the miscreants."

Gladstone sighed. "Yes, Your Grace." He paused, pulling free another piece of parchment. "You instructed me to purchase the entire estate holdings."

"Yes."

"Well, the proprietor informed me that he had already sold part of it off."

"Damn," Nicholas caused. "Which part?"

"The contents of the stables, milord."

"Can you track them?"

Gladstone lifted the paper. "I already have."

"Good man. Buy them back."

"But Your Grace—"

"Buy them back."

On the rare occasions that he attended Almack's he always felt like a fox to the hounds because of all the mamas
who seemed to feel that the assembly was the place for
their daughters to catch a husband. Even so, this evening he
was tempted. There was no use in trying to make excuses.
Surprising though it was, he wanted to see Kate again. The
chit was beautiful, but she was far from the type of female
who generally attracted him. She was outspoken, argumen-
tative, and outrageous. And, he was forced to admit, quite
the most diverting woman he had encountered in years. After much swearing and the destruction of three cravats, to
the dismay of his valet, he took himself off to White's instead.

When he returned sometime after midnight he went
through his mail and found a scrawled invitation from
Thomas to go riding in Hyde Park the next day. He hesitated before writing his answer, for Hyde Park in the early
afternoon was worse than Almack's. But Katherine would
likely be going as well. Damn the woman, anyway, for
making him feel such a nodcock.

Finally he sat back and grinned. She had a quick tongue,
but he doubted she had the experience to back it up. He
scribbled back a reply to the viscount to be delivered in
the morning. He was no green stripling, and he would see
who won this battle.

Mr. Hodges's man had not yet returned from Staffordshire, and there was no word from her uncle, either, despite three additional letters. To Kate's surprise, though,
her godparents, who had been so concerned before, no
longer seemed concerned over Uncle Simon's reticence.

"You cannot assume the worst, Kate," Lady Alison said
as the three of them lunched together. "After all, he is
your uncle."

"We know what a terrible time it was for you," Lord

Neville added soothingly. "Perhaps you exaggerate just a little."

Katherine stood. "I do not exaggerate," she retorted, her temper flaring. "If it were your home at stake, you would feel the same." She grabbed her riding gloves. "I think I should go back to Crestley and see for myself what he is up to."

Lord Neville rose as well. "Nonsense, Kate. You couldn't go on your own."

"I made it here on my own," she reminded him.

"By mail stage," he pointed out.

Katherine shuddered, for she had detested every moment of that smelly, bumpy ride. "I will not let him steal what belongs to me."

"My dear, I will not see you so distressed," Lady Alison said, reaching up to take her hand. Kate didn't see the scathing look she shot at her husband.

"Kate, I will send someone to look into matters at Crestley," Lord Neville said quickly. "There is no need for you to go. Will that suffice?"

"I already—" Kate swallowed. They would both be hurt if she admitted to going behind their backs. It seemed she had plunked herself into a hole. But perhaps Lord Neville would get a quicker response than she had been able to muster. "All right," she agreed, nodding.

Shortly after that Louisa and Thomas arrived to escort her to Hyde Park. Again the viscount was more than generous in his praise of her, but his kind words affected her far less than did the erratic compliments of the Black Duke. It shouldn't have been so, for half the time she wasn't certain if Sommesby even meant what he said, and the other half of the time what he said provoked her beyond bearing. If only he would stop being so unpredictable, there was no doubt she would tire of thinking about him, and dreaming about him, almost immediately.

When they arrived at the park the Black Duke himself was present, seated on a great black charger and conversing amiably with the captain. She found her eyes focusing on his lips, and her thoughts on the intoxicating kiss he had given her the day before. Unsettled, she came near to claiming a headache and returning to the Hamptons' before he saw her. She didn't, however, telling herself that if she did leave he would likely drive poor Althaea, already cowering on the far side of her brother, to another fit of the vapors.

At that moment he turned and smiled. He kneed his stallion forward, stopping beside her to lean over and pat her mare's neck. "Hello, Winter," he said amiably, and the gray's ears flicked at him. When Kate looked back at his face, his eyes were on her. "Katherine," he said, inclining his head.

So he would greet her horse first, would he? "Nicholas," she returned coolly. "You seem to be familiar with my mount, sir."

"I am," he replied mildly. "I sold her to Neville several weeks ago."

That would have been about the time she arrived in London. Her godfather had never said he had purchased Winter specifically for her, only that he thought he had a mare in his stable that would suit her. And he had never mentioned that the gray had come from the Duke of Sommesby.

They set off along the main drag, their progress slower than usual because of the unprecedented appearance of the Black Duke at such a heavily trafficked hour. It seemed that every carriage or chaise, especially those containing women, had to stop and hail him with a word or a greeting. Katherine would have thought he was deliberately baiting her again, except that she caught the bored expression on his face, quickly masked, during a lull. She wondered what it must be like for him to be so badly toadeaten wherever he went in public, and never to know if people's comments and compliments were sincere or merely meant to gain some political or social advantage.

"Do you know everyone in London, Nick?" Thomas finally protested.

"Apparently so," the Black Duke drawled.

"I don't believe it," Louisa muttered from beside Reg.

"What?" the captain asked, turning to follow her gaze.

Katherine looked as well, and her palms grew sweaty inside her gloves. Approaching from across the park on a bay gelding came Francis DuPres. Wishing now that she hadn't spoken so boldly about her ability to take care of herself, she glanced over at Nicholas. To her surprise, he returned her look with a reassuring one of his own. His black sidled closer, seemingly of its own accord.

"Steady," he murmured.

They waited as DuPres closed the distance to them. The close-set brown eyes shifted between her and the duke, as though DuPres couldn't decide which of them warranted his attention. He frightened and revolted Katherine, but she was reassured by the thought that he wouldn't dare try anything in the presence of three high-ranking members of the *ton*.

Finally he settled his attention on Nicholas. "Sommesby, we have something to discuss."

"I have nothing to discuss with you," Nicholas returned icily.

"Ah, but this is not personal," DuPres went on, though the look in his eyes became ugly. "This is business."

"Then make an appointment with my man," the duke responded.

"I've tried. He's never in. And we both know why. It seems that we're both interested in the same property up—"

"I said, make an appointment," Nicholas hissed. As he finished speaking, his black reared. DuPres was forced to haul his bay sideways. The animal whinnied and began crow-hopping. With his high shirt points and harlequin colors, the man looked like a mad elf. "Let's go," the duke said with a growl, and yanked the stallion around.

"That was a bit severe, wasn't it?" Reg asked carefully when they had gone some distance. Behind them DuPres had gotten his horse under control and sat staring after them. After a while he rode off in the opposite direction.

"I didn't come here to discuss business," the duke responded. "And not with the likes of him."

Although Katherine held no liking for Francis DuPres, the duke's attitude of superiority surprised and irked her. "I hadn't realized you were such a high stickler," she said smoothly.

His sharp look set her back. "You would defend him?" he said sharply.

"I am merely pointing out that you seem to be attacking him because his blood isn't as blue as yours."

"You—I—" The Black Duke shut his mouth and glared at her. "I don't give a flying leap about his social status," he said very evenly. "I was attacking him because of his damned ill behavior as a gentleman."

She flushed, her temper flaring. "I believe," she retorted, "that he has behaved no differently than a certain other gentleman with whom we are acquainted."

His eyes narrowed. "You go too far," he said.

"No, sir, you did," Kate replied. Althaea gasped, and Kate gathered her reins to flee as the Black Duke started toward her.

He opened his mouth in a snarl, but before he could say anything Thomas rode between them. "What say we go and get some ices from the confectioner's?" he said loudly. "I think we could all stand to cool down a bit."

This last he directed at Nicholas, and for a moment Katherine thought the Black Duke was going to strike the viscount. Then he slowly nodded, and behind her Reg breathed a sigh of relief.

Conversation was muted as they made their way over to the confectioner's. When Thomas and Nicholas dismounted to get the ices, Louisa leaned over to Kate. "I thought he was going to eat you alive," she whispered. "Now I know why he is called the Black Duke."

Wishing that for once she had possessed enough sense

to keep her mouth shut, Katherine shook her head. "I provoked him," she whispered back.

"Yes, you did," a soft voice came from beside her, and she looked down to see Nicholas standing at her knee. "Again." He held a lemon-flavored ice up in one hand and strawberry in the other. When she indicated the lemon he handed it to her. "And again you put me in my place," he murmured.

"Someone has to," she noted, smiling a little nervously.

He put a hand on her reins and leaned closer. "Then I'm pleased you aren't carrying a vase with you." At that he grinned, the smile lighting his eyes and making her wish to lean down and kiss him, right in the middle of Hyde Park. Drat the man, she didn't know how to behave when he was about.

"Do you go to the Linton soiree tomorrow night?" he asked.

She pulled her thoughts together enough to nod. "I do."

"Will you save a waltz for me?"

So much for his threat never to dance with her again, but she wasn't about to remind him of it. "Yes, I will."

"Are you going to stand there all day, Nick?" Thomas's voice came from behind them, and the duke started.

"I suppose not," he drawled, and with another smile and a faint shrug to her, he returned to his stallion and swung back up into the saddle.

They ate their flavored ices in the shade of a stand of oaks. After another few minutes of listening to Thomas trying to make some kind of bet regarding a rematch between his bay and Nicholas's black, Ulysses, they were all laughing again. Then, too quickly, Sommesby had to take his leave, claiming a business appointment he had been unable to break.

"Miss Dremond, Miss Hillary," he intoned, much to Althaea's trepidation. "Katherine." He touched his heels to the black's ribs and was gone.

They lingered for another half hour before Reg stretched and climbed to his feet. "We should be getting back, as well," he commented, and Althaea rose from her seat in the soft grass.

As Katherine rode beside Thomas and Louisa on the way back to the Hamptons', the viscount kept glancing over at her. He said nothing, though, until he dismounted to walk her to the door. "Kate . . . was Nick forward with you?"

Katherine blushed. "Whatever do you mean?"

"Well, it's just that Nick usually gets his way, and he's used to . . . dealing with ladies of a different sort than you," he said slowly, carefully choosing his words. "If you don't wish his attentions, I will be happy to speak to him for you."

She touched his sleeve and smiled. "Thank you, Thomas, but I can deal with Nicholas Varon myself."

"Yes, you likely can," he muttered.

10

After changing her mind so many times she had begun to think herself addlebrained, Katherine decided to wear her blue gown to the Lintons'. She fidgeted at the dressing table until Emmie set down the hairbrush and suggested she take a stroll and return when she was ready to sit still.

"I'm sorry, Emmie," she apologized, turning to face forward again.

"You're in high spirits tonight, Miss Kate, ain't you?" Emmie queried, lifting the brush again.

Katherine picked up the silver hair ribbon and began to wind it around her fingers, then quickly put it down again when Emmie sighed. "I suppose I am a bit ... jittery this evening," she admitted.

"One of those fine gentlemen finally caught your eye, did he?" The maid dimpled, then grimaced as one of the silver clips fell out of Kate's hair to the floor.

"Heavens, no," Katherine protested weakly. As she realized she was picking at the ribbon again, she folded her hands in her lap. Despite Kate's lack of cooperation, Emmie completed her ministrations and over Kate's protests declared that her mistress was going to be the envy of all London that evening.

At the Linton mansion the throng of male admirers that

beset Kate upon her arrival seemed to agree with Emmie. The Hamptons relinquished her to the crowd, and almost before she could take a breath her card was filled. Except for the last dance. She kept that waltz free, as she had given her word. She looked about for Sommesby, but he was not in sight. Nicholas was not the type to clamor for attention with the other young bucks, though, so she was not unduly concerned.

As the evening progressed and he still had made no appearance, however, her temper began to flare. He wouldn't be so petty as to stand her up in revenge for her walking out early the night they had met, or so she told herself. Once the thought entered her mind, however, it refused to depart. She had behaved like a hoyden out in the park, and he could be so devious that she would put nothing past him, the scoundrel. "Oh, fribble," she muttered.

"Beg pardon?"

She looked up to see the Viscount of Sheresford standing before her, and smiled. "Oh, hello, Thomas."

He stood for another moment, then sat down beside her. "Do you wish to sit out this dance?" he asked, and she remembered that he had claimed her for the quadrille.

She shook her head. "No. I'm sorry. I've just been distracted tonight."

"The belle of the ball is allowed to be as distracted as she pleases, for she is very distracting to most everyone else." Thomas grinned and pulled her to her feet.

"I am not the belle of the ball," she stated as they took their places.

"Look around, if you don't believe me," he suggested as the music began.

She did so, and found that she was receiving a great deal more attention than she had realized. "I did not try to be so," she protested as they stepped forward. "It's not even my debut. I've had my Season."

Thomas laughed. "You are too generous," he said. "Enjoy it. Before long you will be off the market, and some other young miss will take your place."

As the dance separated them, she considered his words. His attentions had become more serious of late, and it occurred to her that he might offer for her. She was quite fond of him, but she had heard complaints about her Irish temper often enough that she well knew it was entirely likely he would become exasperated with her stubborn ways and not offer for her at all.

After the quadrille ended he led her over to Lord Neville, her partner for the next-to-last dance of the evening, a country dance. "I shall try not to step on your toes, dear," her godfather said with a grin as she returned to the floor.

"You are a fine dancer," she returned stoutly, again glancing about the room for Nicholas. Abruptly she spied him lounging in the doorway, watching her. He nodded at her, and she sighed, relieved that he had come, after all. As she and Lord Neville left the floor he started toward them. He was dressed in a blue even darker than her own, his cravat as white as snow. He looked magnificent, and seemed to draw the eye of everyone in the room as he approached.

"Neville," he said, inclining his head to the baron before bending to take Kate's hand and kiss her knuckle. "Katherine," he murmured, then straightened. "Have I missed our dance?"

"Very nearly," she returned, and the waltz began.

The duke swept her out onto the floor. This time as they swirled about to the music his expression did not become bored, and, rather than wander about the room, his gaze remained on her as she looked up at him. "I'm sorry I was so late," he apologized.

"It was quite dramatic of you," she returned.

"I truly intended to arrive less dramatically an hour ago," he responded. "I had another meeting I couldn't break." He looked down at her skeptical expression. "Don't look daggers at me, Kate. If you must know, I and several others were asked to meet with Cousin Prinny and the prime minister. The Marquis of Belning was there as well, so you can ask Reg if you don't believe me."

"*Cousin* Prinny?" she repeated, raising an eyebrow.

"Yes, of sorts. Didn't you know?" At her head shake he leaned closer. "I am lucky thirteenth in line to the throne," he murmured.

"You're bamming me," she replied, eyeing him uncertainly.

"I am not," he protested. "Father and old King George were second cousins, or some such thing."

She did finally believe him, though she had had no idea that the Duke of Sommesby's very blue blood was that blue. "Well, m'lord, you've missed a lovely evening," she said, conveniently forgetting the fact that she had been irked at him for not appearing.

"I don't know about that," he returned. "Thomas looked none too happy when I arrived."

"He says I'm the belle of the ball," she responded, more to bait the duke than because she believed it.

Nicholas nodded. "Oh."

"Well," she prompted, annoyed, "aren't you going to say anything nice?"

"Last time I tried to give you a compliment you gave me a set-down," he drawled. "I'm not certain I want to risk it again."

"Gammon," she retorted. "You don't want to give me a compliment because you are the most irritating, selfish, provoking man alive."

He laughed. Katherine noted again that they seemed to be the center of attention, and she frowned. "Oh, stop it," she muttered.

That only made him laugh harder. "And you still want a compliment after that?" He chuckled, his eyes full of dancing green highlights. "Well, then, m'dear, 'Shall I compare thee to a summer's day? Thou art more lovely and more—' "

"Don't you dare say it, Nicholas Varon," she warned,

biting her lip to keep the determined frown from sliding from her face.

He pursed his lips as though deep in thought, and then nodded. "I think you're right. 'Temperate' does not suit you. 'Tempestuous,' perhaps." He gazed down at her. "Or impossibly lovely, with eyes a man could drown in."

The compliment, when it finally came, was so unexpected and so softly said that for an instant she couldn't speak. "Well, perhaps I was a bit harsh a moment ago," she muttered, and he chuckled again.

At the end of the waltz he returned her to the Hamptons and greeted both of them. The duke rubbed his hands together and glanced about. "Katherine, would you like to accompany me on a drive to the country tomorrow?" He turned to the baroness. "With your approval, of course, Alison."

"And who would be escorting you?" her godmother asked, eyeing him. "I won't have any scandal attached to Kate."

Nicholas shook his head. "Neither would I. I know my reputation." His expression changed a little, making Kate wonder if perhaps the infamous Black Duke wasn't as uncaring about his reputation as he appeared. "I'll take Jack along. I've known him all my life, and I haven't yet ruined anyone in his presence. Will that suffice?"

Her godmother nodded. "Your groom will be fine. If Kate wants to go."

Feeling a bit left out of the conversation, Katherine looked back up at Nicholas. He raised an eyebrow at her. "Yes, I would love to."

She was coming down the stairs as Rawlins opened the front door to admit the Duke of Sommesby. Kate resisted the urge to brush at her peach walking dress, but couldn't help her smile as he approached the foot of the stairs and waited there for her.

He took both of her hands in his and raised them to his

lips. "Good morning, Katherine. Am I permitted to say that you look lovely?"

He was baiting her, and so she nodded regally. "Yes," she answered.

"You look lovely, Katherine," he repeated dutifully, continuing to hold her hands in his long-fingered ones.

"Nick," Lord Neville said as he came out of the morning room. He cleared his throat as he saw them standing together, and Katherine tried to pull away. Nicholas tightened his grip in response. "Excuse me," her godfather continued, "but might I have a word with you when you return?"

The duke nodded. "Of course." He returned his gaze to Katherine. "Shall we go?"

He took her shawl from Rawlins and put it around her shoulders himself, then took her parasol and led her outside. They were to take the high-perch phaeton, she realized with delight. A magnificent-looking team of matched grays waited, held by a small, gray-haired man with a moustache and a pair of merry, light-blue eyes.

"Do you like roast chicken?" the duke asked, helping her into the high seat and then thumping the basket stowed behind her as he circled around the rig and climbed up next to her.

"Yes." She nodded, watching as the groom released the horses and stepped back. Nicholas touched the reins, and the team sprang forward. As the rig passed by him, the groom swung up behind them, next to the picnic basket.

"This is our nanny, Jack," Nicholas told her, nodding in the groom's direction.

"Good morning, miss," Jack greeted her, doffing his cap and grinning.

"Good morning, Jack," she answered, smiling back at him.

The duke had to hold the team back the entire time they were in London, and she couldn't help but admire his skillful maneuvering of the spirited pair. She had heard the

Black Duke could drive to an inch, and saw no reason to disbelieve the claim.

As they left the city behind, the grays moved into a canter. There was little traffic as they traveled through the green countryside, and Katherine found herself smiling as they drove along. She had missed being in the country.

"There's a spot I have in mind," Nicholas said, "about an hour from here." He looked over at her. "What are you smiling at?"

She shrugged, looking back at him. "I'm happy," she admitted.

He grinned. "You are easy to please," he replied.

"May I try?" she asked, motioning at the reins and attempting to take advantage of his good humor.

He lifted an eyebrow at her. "Have you driven before?" he asked dubiously.

"I used to drive my father's team quite a bit before he was killed," she answered. "He said I was good."

Nicholas glanced at the empty road ahead of them again and shrugged. "Brace your feet," he advised, "or they'll pull you right over."

She did as he said, and he handed over the reins. He was right; the team was still fresh, and, seeming to sense a new driver, strained against her. She braced her shoulders and kept the horses to a canter, enjoying their liveliness and the feel of them responding to her light commands. After a league or so a milk wagon appeared, coming toward them, but Nicholas sat back and crossed his arms.

Katherine grinned and, determined not to embarrass herself by running the phaeton into the hedge at the side of the road, clucked to the team and guided it over to one side of the way. The wagon passed them without incident, the driver doffing his hat to her.

"Your father was right. You're a fine whip." Nicholas chuckled.

He let her drive until her arms grew tired, then took the ribbons back. Finally he guided the phaeton off the road under a stand of elms. A short walk from the lane, a small brook ran through a shady meadow. Jack climbed down and went to the horses while Nicholas tied the ribbons and jumped to the ground. He came around to lift Katherine down, placing his hands on her waist. His touch made her feel breathless, and he held her longer than he needed, looking down at her.

"Hungry?" he asked finally, and when she nodded he released her and pulled the picnic basket off the back of the rig. She took his free arm, and they walked through the lush grass to the edge of the water.

Nicholas set out a blanket in the shade and then sat cross-legged beside her. He handed her two glasses and poured Madeira into them, then took one back from her. "To a day in the country," he toasted, and she smiled and clinked the fine crystal against his.

"And to a fine team of horses," she added, and he laughed and raised his glass again.

Still smiling, he tilted the glass at her. "And to you." He took a sip, looking at her over the rim, and then set the glass aside to delve into the hamper. "Oh. This is for you," he said, and handed her a small box tied with a bright-blue ribbon.

She glanced up at him suspiciously, then accepted the package when she could read nothing more than amusement in his gaze. Carefully she untied the ribbon and pulled off the lid. Seeing the contents, she burst into laughter. "You remembered," she chortled, and lifted out a chocolate cream to pop it into her mouth.

"Of course," he replied, chuckling as he accepted one of the candies.

She watched as he prepared her a plate of roast chicken and handed it over. "How often does the Duke of Sommesby go on picnics?" she asked.

He glanced up at her and shrugged in a very un-Black Duke-like manner. "Not very often," he replied, removing his hat and jacket and setting them aside.

"And why is that?" she pursued, trying not to focus her

attention on how dashing he looked in his waistcoat and shirtsleeves.

He shrugged again and grinned, taking a slice of peach and then offering her one. "No challenge."

Kate didn't know quite how to reply to that, and so she took a moment to remove her irksome bonnet and dump it on the blanket. "I take it, then, that you find me to be a challenge?" she returned.

"I find you infinitely challenging," the duke responded. "In fact, I have made it my personal quest to determine what motivates you."

"I thought we had that conversation," she replied, blushing. It was the first time he had actually intimated that he was interested in her, that he found her more than merely amusing, as she had half begun to fear. Kate glanced down at the gift he had given her and smiled, lifting it in one hand. "Remember?"

He laughed. "I believe you did mention several other things that were at least as important to you as chocolate creams." Nicholas glanced down at his plate, and set it aside. "You said that your father had been killed," he said quietly, his smile fading. "Do you mind my asking what happened?"

She shook her head. "We had just come to London for my Season, and he had to go home on business. On the way back to town his carriage slid off the road during a rainstorm, and he was trapped beneath it and drowned." After two years she could speak of it in a steady voice, but the news, when it came, had been devastating.

"I'm sorry," he said softly. "How come you to Neville and Alison after all this time?"

"My mother died seven months ago of pneumonia," she answered, glancing away.

Nicholas sat up straighter. "Why didn't you say anything?"

"What was I supposed to say?" she returned, touched by the compassion in his voice. "Mama forbade me to go into mourning. She said it was time for me to live." She shrugged and smiled. "You've certainly made it easier for me to forget."

He laughed again. "I have become notorious for making women forget things at opportune times," he drawled.

She blushed, for she could imagine what he was implying. "No doubt," she answered, looking straight at him and refusing to let him think he had shocked her.

He leaned toward her, and she found herself tilting her head sideways. The duke paused for a moment, his expression telling her that he knew exactly what she was thinking, then reached a hand over and brushed at her lower lip with one finger. "You have a little chocolate on . . ."

Embarrassed, she raised a hand to wipe it away, but he grasped her fingers and pulled her toward him with practiced ease. "Your Grace—" she started to say.

"I'll take care of it," he murmured, and kissed her.

Her arms went around his shoulders as if of their own accord, and he chuckled against her mouth and shifted forward to kiss her again. He pushed her over backward, his weight settling across her hip and pinning her beneath him. Kate was breathless and tingling all over, her heart pounding so hard, she thought he must be able to feel it against his chest.

A figure stepped up to block the filtered sunlight. "Excuse me, Your Grace."

Nicholas let Kate go as though he had been scalded, and sat upright. "Damn," he muttered, staring down at her, then turned to look up at Jack, standing a few feet away. "Jack, consider yourself dismissed."

"Yes, Your Grace."

Katherine, her face hot, sat up as well. Despite the difficulty she was still having with breathing, she wasn't certain she was grateful for the groom's interference either; he had likely saved her virtue, but at that moment she didn't know if she wanted her virtue saved. She watched Nicholas's profile closely, after a moment unable to help smiling at the exchange that followed.

"Don't you have to water the horses?"

"Did that, Your Grace."

"Walk them?" Reluctant amusement began to war with the frustration on Nicholas's face.

"Did that, Your Grace."

"Go away, Jack."

"Can't do that, Your Grace."

"Well, we can," the duke stated, rising to his feet. He held a hand down and pulled her up after him. He reached down again and handed her the parasol before he placed her hand over his arm. Without a backward glance he led her along the creek. After a moment he looked down at her. "Again you make me forget myself. Baiting me can be a dangerous thing for a young lady to do."

"Yes," she answered, again unwilling to let him cow her. "I know."

He shook his head. "Damn it, Katherine! I'm not used to this kind of game, and I'm afraid I don't play it very well."

"Thomas said as much," she replied, swinging her parasol back and forth in her hand and wondering what kind of game he thought he was playing with her, and what winning it would entail.

"What exactly did Thomas say?" the Black Duke queried, his tone sharper.

"Only that you were used to a different kind of woman than I. He implied that I might need rescuing."

"He's right. On both counts." He stopped and moved in front of her. "You've likely heard a great many things about me," he said slowly, his gray eyes serious, "and most of them are probably true. Some things I did simply because I could, because there was no one willing to try to stop me." He paused for a moment, then smiled. "And believe me, you are the first person to ever accuse me of being a high stickler."

She grinned back. "I can believe that."

He laughed, taking her hand to raise it to his lips. "I am pleased you came to London this Season," he murmured, chuckling, and, still holding her hand, started to move forward again.

She remembered what she had heard about how dubiously he had begun the summer. The Black Duke before her little resembled the rakehell she had heard discussed. "I miss home a little, but so am I."

"Where is home?"

"A tiny estate a few days north of here." She pursed her lips ruefully. "I daresay Crestley is probably smaller than your stables at Sommesby."

His hand jumped in hers. "Crestley?" he repeated slowly.

"Mm-hm. Crestley Hall. You should see it. It's so beautiful. Mama loved roses, and the whole garden blooms all summer. I used to love to open my window in the evening and let the smell of the flowers inside my room." Nicholas didn't say anything, and she thought she must be boring him. "I'm sorry if I'm prattling."

He looked over at her, his expression more solemn than she would have expected. "I have yet to hear you prattle, Kate. Crestley sounds enchanting."

She sighed when Nicholas finally glanced down at his pocket watch. "I would hate to have put up with all of this to preserve your reputation and then ruin you by keeping you out after dark," he muttered with a glance at his groom as they turned back, and she laughed again.

They loaded the remains of their picnic back into the hamper, which Nicholas carried back to the phaeton. While he put it away she walked up to where Jack stood holding the horses. "These are beautiful animals," she said.

"Aye," Jack agreed, "and His Grace is real particular about who holds the ribbons. Only him 'n' me ever driven 'em before today."

She looked at the groom closely, finding that piece of information very interesting. "Why is—"

"Ready to go?" Nicholas asked, coming up beside her. She wasn't, but nodded as he helped her up into the high seat. *"The Magic Flute* comes to the opera next week," he said, moving around and climbing up beside her. "You and the Hamptons would be welcome to join me in my box."

She nodded, grinning. "That would be grand." After a moment she laughed.

"What now?" he asked, clucking at the team.

"You sounded so . . . proper," she said with a chuckle.

Nicholas looked over at her and furrowed his brow. "There's no need to be insulting," he returned. He faced forward for a moment, then snorted and glanced sideways at her. " 'Proper'? Now I'm offended," he muttered.

Katherine just laughed at him.

The Duke of Sommesby had never spent such a day in his life, and didn't quite know what to make of what had transpired. On rare occasions he had been induced to take one or other of his mistresses picnicking, but even with the complete license they granted him, he had not felt what he had experienced by sharing one afternoon, and one kiss, with Katherine Ralston. Just when he thought he was winning the battle she changed the rules, and he had no idea what to do with her.

Over the past few weeks it had finally begun to occur to him that perhaps his own reputation did matter, and not simply for his own sake. If he saw Katherine again it would begin to reflect on her. And he did want to see her again, with an urge so strong he felt powerless to resist. His mind and his heart had begun behaving like two different entities, leaving him dazed and befuddled with so many conflicting emotions he was halfway to believing he had gone mad and might as well sit back and enjoy the ride.

He stopped the phaeton outside Hampton House and came around to hand Katherine down. With a word to Jack to keep the horses standing, he followed her to the door. As though sensing their presence, Rawlins swung the door open, but Kate stopped on the top step. "I wanted to thank you," she murmured, and touched his sleeve. "I had a splendid time."

He took her hand and raised it to his lips. "As did I," he answered with what was likely a rather addlepated smile.

She looked up at him for a long moment, her blue eyes twinkling, and then stepped inside. With a deep sigh and a silent curse at all diligent grooms, he followed. He watched her go upstairs, then found Neville in his office.

"Nick," the baron said in acknowledgment, but the duke thought the greeting sounded cool.

He could guess why, and he had his own reasons for being annoyed with Clarey in return. "Neville," he replied, shutting the office door and taking a seat.

"Did you have a pleasant time?"

Nicholas nodded. "Yes. Thank you."

The baron stood, walked around the office, then sat down again. "She's like a daughter to me, you know," he burst out.

"I know," Nicholas answered, making what he deemed an admirable effort at keeping his temper. "I'm glad she had somewhere to go when she left Crestley."

Clarey started and looked up at him. "Nick—"

Sommesby stood. "I don't know what's going on," he said with a growl, "but consider me out of it." He turned for the door.

"Sommesby, it's not what you think. I would never hurt Kate."

Nicholas stopped with his hand on the door. "Then why am I buying her estate out from under her? She has no idea, Neville."

"I know. It's her damned uncle. The man's never done an honest day's work in his life, but he was named Kate's guardian. The first thing the bastard did was to send Kate here, then put Crestley up for sale as soon as she was out the door." Neville looked at him. "Or so I assume."

Somewhat reassured by the baron's obvious indignation,

Nicholas released the door handle and turned around. "You're right. It came on the market."

"You see now why I couldn't become involved, why I needed—"

"A rakehell with a bad enough reputation that Kate's uncle would believe I would willingly cheat her out of her inheritance?" He shook his head, trying to curb his anger at himself, Neville, and, mostly, Kate's dear uncle. "Some things are too dastardly even for me."

"Nick, I don't know what else to do. Simon Ralston would burn Crestley to the ground before he'd walk away from it."

Nicholas closed his eyes for a moment, then jabbed a finger at the baron. "You tell Katherine about this. She loves Crestley. She deserves to know." Besides, he thought, she'd likely kill him if she suspected he was hiding something from her; also, although he thrived on upsetting and annoying people, hurting her was the last thing he wanted to do.

"I'll tell her."

"All right." He nodded and took a deep breath. "I believe I'm close to striking a deal. My man should be back in a day or two. I'll inform you as soon as I find out myself."

Neville stood. "Thank you, Nick."

Nicholas shook his head and rose as well. "Thank me when the deal's done."

11

🍇

Katherine awoke to the scent of roses. After a dreamy moment she started, then sat up to see Emmie placing a large vase filled with several dozen red and white blooms on her dressing table. "What's this?" she queried.

"Oh, Miss Kate, these come for you first thing this morning. I wanted them to be here when you woke up," her maid gushed. "Ain't they grand?"

"They are." Katherine smiled as she spied the note settled among the buds.

"Shall I bring you up your morning tea, miss?" Emmie went over to the window and drew back the curtains, letting in the morning sunlight.

"Yes, please."

As soon as Emmie had shut the door behind her, Katherine dashed over to the flowers. She leaned forward and breathed deeply of their fresh scent, then pulled out the envelope. Her name was written boldly across the front, and she smiled. The typically brief missive made her laugh. It said, "To a fine whip. Nicholas."

She was still smiling when she came down to breakfast, to find that her godparents had just sat down as well. "Good morning," she greeted them, going around the table to kiss each of them on the cheek.

"Good morning, m'dear," Lord Neville responded, though he seemed a little subdued.

"Have you sent someone to Crestley?" she asked, abruptly remembering that he had promised to do so.

He nodded and finished spreading jam on his toast. "We should hear in a few days how things stand there," he informed her, then cleared his throat. "Kate—"

She could guess what he was going to say, and didn't want to end up explaining that she had gone behind his back. Not when she was in such a good mood that morning. "I appreciate your assistance, but I do mean to handle this myself. If anything has happened at Crestley, I will deal with it."

There was a moment of silence. "Kate, there's something—"

She raised a hand. "Please, Lord Neville. I am serious."

Lady Alison cleared her throat. "You received more roses this morning."

"Yes, I did," she responded, her smile returning.

"Were they from Nick?"

She nodded, accepting the jar of marmalade from her godfather. "Thank you. Yes, they were."

Lady Alison leaned across the table, her face serious. "Kate, Nick is a dear friend, but he does have a certain reputation. We don't wish to see you hurt."

Katherine was touched by their concern, though she felt it to be unnecessary. "He has made no declaration to me," she said, "other than to invite the three of us to the opera next week."

Alison nudged her husband. "He's been chased by so many mothers and their eligible daughters that he has informed me on several occasions that he has sworn off marriage entirely," Lord Neville said with a forced smile.

"How do you feel about him, child?" her godmother asked.

"I think he is very provoking," Katherine answered truthfully.

Her godparents seemed unsatisfied with her answer, but

she couldn't give them a better one. She thought she was beginning to like him more than she was comfortable admitting even to herself, but then he had been going out of his way to be charming. She knew as well as anyone that at any time the Black Duke could become bored with her, or find someone else to engage his rather jaded attention.

That evening she and the Hamptons had been asked to dinner at the Hillary mansion, and Reg had mentioned that Nicholas had been invited as well. Katherine hoped he would attend, so that she could thank him for the roses, and for the moment of memories they had brought.

The Marquis of Belning was a large, jolly man, as one would have to be in a household with seven lively offspring. His wife, Jane, was equally rotund, but the task of finding husbands for her three daughters had left her with considerably less humor. When Katherine and her godparents arrived they found Thomas there already, along with Louisa and Robert Albey, a school chum of Reg's younger brother Thad. Shortly afterward they all repaired to the household's large dining room. As the first course was being served the butler came in to announce His Grace, Nicholas Varon, the Duke of Sommesby.

At the pronouncement Nicholas strolled into the room. The emerald green superfine jacket and waistcoat he wore made his eyes glint. The captain came away from the table to shake his hand, and then the duke made his way over to greet the marquis and gracefully bow to the marchioness.

"Oh, dear," Althaea muttered in a miserable voice from across the table, and Katherine hid a smile with her napkin.

"You grace our table, er, Your Grace," the marquis rumbled.

That produced a round of laughter from the younger set. As Nicholas turned to take his seat, his amused glance met Katherine's, and he inclined his head. After a noisy, boisterous supper the women repaired to the drawing room while the marquis called for port. Katherine found herself, as usual, sitting with Louisa and Althaea.

"Oh, he never comes to these house parties," Althaea complained. "Reg has invited him a hundred times."

"Don't fret, Thaea," Louisa said comfortingly, sending Kate an amused look. "Perhaps his other plans were canceled. The Black Duke wouldn't want to sit at home."

"But now Mama will expect me to converse with him," the brown-eyed beauty said with a moan. "And I will say something foolish, and he will give me a good setdown. I know he will."

At that moment Katherine felt someone's eyes on her, and turned to see Nicholas come into the room, a glass of port in one hand. Seeing seven pairs of female eyes on him, he flashed a smile. "I have always thought it a rather foolish custom," he drawled, coming to seat himself next to Louisa, "that men stay huddled together in the dining room after supper when just next door, beautiful women wait to be entertained."

Katherine thought it a typically haughty thing for him to say, but it seemed to greatly impress Althaea's younger sisters and her mama, while it prompted another groan from the girl herself. Led by Thomas, the rest of the men appeared a moment later, and they became a party of sixteen. After a few minutes of increasingly noisy conversation the marchioness suggested in a loud voice that Althaea play them something on the pianoforte.

The viscount moved to take the girl's vacated seat next to Katherine, and she caught the quick look that passed between him and Nicholas as Althaea began to play. "She plays well," Kate whispered to Thomas, and he nodded.

"Do you play?" he returned.

She frowned. "What's the standard reply? Adequately?" In truth she had no patience for it, and had escaped from her instructor to go riding whenever she could get away with it.

Althaea played two pieces, but when her mother encouraged her to play a third, her siblings suggested they play charades instead. Althaea gratefully left the pianoforte. "That was beautifully done, Miss Hillary," the Black Duke said amiably as she took a seat.

Althaea blanched and nodded, mumbling something unintelligible. Kate had noticed that the rest of the young people looked at the Duke of Sommesby with something close to awe, and even his close friends, such as Thomas and Reg, showed him a healthy respect. She looked over at Nicholas again. He was smiling now, and looking devilishly handsome, not at all like the black-tempered rogue of ill repute. Seeming to sense her gaze, he glanced over at her and grinned.

Althaea and Louisa took charge in organizing the game, and the young people were instructed to divide into two teams. Katherine stood, and found her elbow gripped by the viscount, who smiled down at her.

"Teammates?" he queried, and she nodded, returning his smile. They had played before, and he was quite good.

Abruptly Nicholas was at her other side, though she hadn't been aware of his approach. Though the Black Duke didn't touch her, his look at Thomas made it clear that he had no intention of leaving her side, and Katherine began to feel something like a wishbone.

"Excuse me, but a Mr. Gladstone is here to see His Grace," the Hillarys' butler announced from the doorway.

"Damn," Nicholas muttered from beside her. "Gerald, may I borrow your study for a moment?" he queried.

"Of course, Your Grace," the marquis returned.

"Best start without me," Nicholas said to the other players, and with a quick grimace of apology strode out of the room, the butler in his wake. Katherine looked after him, then joined the general cheering and talking as a member of each team chose a word out of a bowl to begin the game. Althaea's team won the first round, thanks mostly to her sister Eunice, and then it was Louisa's turn. After the next set of clues the duke returned. He looked somber, and nodded at Lord Neville as he took his seat.

"Is everything all right?" Katherine asked while Thad

Hillary rooted around on the floor, obviously imitating a pig, though his teammates seemed willing to let him suffer for a few moments before they guessed the word.

Nicholas nodded. "Yes." He reached out as though to take her hand, then glanced about and straightened his jacket instead. "It will be—"

"Your turn, Nick," Thomas said, leaning forward and tipping the bowl in Sommesby's direction.

Nicholas gave him an annoyed glance, then with a sigh pulled out one of the pieces of paper. He grimaced, raising an eyebrow. "Can't I choose again?" he asked, reaching for the bowl.

Reg rose and pulled it out of the way. "You get to act as foolish as the rest of us," he said, grinning.

"If this is what being proper gets one, I prefer being a scoundrel," Nicholas whispered to Kate, then stood as she chuckled.

What he had said surprised her. She had suspected as much, but it seemed that he actually was making an effort to behave. The only question was, for what reason; yet as she watched him give the sign for a person and then bend over and cup his hands above his ears, she thought that perhaps she could guess.

"A rabbit?" Louisa asked.

"It's a person," Cecilia Hillary corrected her.

He nodded, lifting two fingers, then resumed his posture in a slightly more upright position.

"Two words," Thomas said, and the duke nodded again.

"Bunny rabbit." Across the room, Reg was chortling.

With a put-upon glance at Kate, Nicholas continued meandering around the furniture. "Donkey?" she queried, trying not to laugh.

"Thank God," he muttered, and straightened.

"No talking," Reg rebuked him.

"That's not a person," Eunice protested.

"That's one word," Louisa crowed.

Nicholas paused for a moment, then wiped his hand across his forehead.

"Tired," Louisa said immediately.

"Warm?" Thomas tried, when that didn't get a response.

The duke's gesture was expansive, his eyes twinkling though his expression was exasperated.

"Hot?" Robert Albey offered.

The duke nodded and folded his arms, obviously finished. While the others called out various and hilarious combinations of the two words, Kate looked at him. He clearly felt that he had given them all of the information they needed, and, considering what she knew of him, the answer was one that was likely so obvious they would all feel foolish for not getting it. "Well?" he mouthed at her, raising an eyebrow.

"Donkey hot," she murmured. "Donkey hot."

"Lord Vincent Westerhill, Third Earl of Malbury," Thomas said.

"What?" Nicholas and Katherine exclaimed in unison.

"He's fat and sweaty, and has about as much intelligence as a donkey," the viscount explained, and Katherine chuckled.

"I'll let him know you said that," Nicholas commented.

"Time's nearly up," Thad Hillary exclaimed, eyeing the clock on the mantel.

Abruptly it came to her, and she sat straight up, smiling gleefully. "Don Quixote," she said triumphantly.

"Bravo," Nicholas murmured through the general cheering and protests. "May I take a seat now?"

By the end of the evening Kate's cheeks felt stretched from laughing so much. No one had any idea which team had actually won, and finally the Marquis of Belning declared the match a draw. Katherine had never seen Nicholas so relaxed and charming, and wondered that anyone could think to be afraid of him.

It was past midnight when she and the Hamptons finally collected their outer garments to leave, and Nicholas followed them out to where the coaches had been brought up. "May I call on you in the morning, Neville?" he asked, handing Lady Alison and then Kate up into the coach. "I don't think we should talk here."

"Of course," the baron answered, throwing a curious, uneasy look at Kate.

The duke looked up into the dark coach at her. "Good night, Katherine," he said softly, sounding warm and intimate enough to make her blush.

"Good night, Nicholas," she replied, smiling.

Kate had her own caller in the morning. Emmie awoke her at nine to say that a Mr. Hodges was waiting for her in the morning room. "Oh, dear," she murmured, and dressed quickly to meet him. This was surely what she had been waiting for, and she was both anxious and reluctant to hear the news he carried.

"Mr. Hodges," she said, entering the room and closing the door.

"Miss Ralston," he replied, setting aside his satchel and coming to his feet. "I know you prefer to meet in my offices, but my man only returned last evening, and I thought you would want his news immediately."

"Yes, thank you," she answered, motioning him to resume his seat. She was too nervous to sit, herself, and tried not to squeeze her hands together. "What did he discover?"

He cleared his throat and reached into the satchel. "No estate is officially up for sale in Staffordshire," he began, pulling out a piece of parchment and handing it to her, "but representatives of these parties have all been to Crestley Hall in the past few weeks. I must preface this by saying that the following is purely conjecture, but the offer of the party at the bottom of the list, the name I've circled, was apparently accepted three days ago."

While he was speaking Katherine perused the paper. Most of the names were unfamiliar to her, but even so, she felt she was looking at a list of her worst enemies. Francis DuPres's name was fourth from the top, and for a brief moment she was grateful that it was not he whom she would have to battle for her home. The circled name at the bottom, though, stopped her cold. "Are you certain of this?" she whispered, her voice cracking. Feeling abruptly faint, she sat down on the couch.

"Yes, my man was quite certain. As far as we know, no funds have changed hands yet, so we still have time to file a motion in court." He looked down, clearing his throat again. "However, considering who you are apparently up against, I really don't—"

"No. No," Katherine whispered, staring at the list. No wonder Nicholas had been so attentive to her. He had wanted to make certain she didn't suspect anything. "I shall take care of this, Mr. Hodges." She made her way to the door, opening it and motioning him out. "Please send me your bill."

"Miss Ralston, I would be more than—"

"Please, Mr. Hodges. I will handle it."

The solicitor picked up his things and walked to the door, then hesitated. "I'm quite sorry," he muttered, and bowed to her. "Good day, milady."

"Thank you," Kate replied numbly. As soon as he was gone she rushed upstairs into her bedchamber and slammed the door shut behind her.

She was not surprised that her uncle had somehow found a way to sell off Crestley Hall, for she had suspected all along that he would attempt something like that. But Nicholas had betrayed her. He had danced with her, teased with her, and sent her roses. She looked at the beautiful arrangement sitting on her dressing table, then without ceremony turned it upside down into the chamber pot.

He had thought to outsmart her, had he? Well, he would find that task not as easy as he obviously expected. He had done it before, the blackguard, and she should have realized what he was up to. He had taken the Viscount of Worton's estate during a card game, and now he sought to steal Crestley from her. But he would not. No money had changed hands. She could still stop him.

Kate paced the room. Nicholas was going to pay for his

behavior. He couldn't make her care for him and then steal from her, especially after she had told him how much she loved Crestley. He was far too wealthy for her to be able to buy him off, but maybe she could otherwise convince him to back out of the purchase. He was so certain that he had her wound around his little finger. He probably even thought she had fallen in love with him. Well, she would use that. She would use his own arrogance and pride against him. She would show Nicholas Varon.

The clock on the stair landing chimed nine forty-five. He would be there at any moment to meet with Lord Neville. Before she had time to change her mind or lose her nerve, she dashed downstairs and found the butler standing in the hallway. "Rawlins," she said, "when the Duke of Sommesby arrives, please send him into the morning room."

"Yes, Miss Kate," he agreed, too well schooled to point out that it was very odd for her to be receiving such a guest alone.

That done, she slipped into Lord Neville's office and found one of his pistols in the bottom desk drawer. Her hand shaking, she removed it and hid it in the folds of her skirt, feeling a need for some security against the duke's infamous black temper. That done, she made her way back into the morning room and waited by the mantel.

She only had to wait for ten minutes before a knock sounded at the front door, and her breath caught in her throat. She heard muffled voices, and then the morning-room door opened. Nicholas entered and looked at her, his expression one of amused pleasure.

"You wanted to see me?" he asked, stepping forward and gazing at her with obvious curiosity.

Involuntarily she took a step back. "Close the door, please."

He did as she asked, then came further into the room. "You wanted to see me . . . alone?" he continued, a wicked smile spreading across his face. "Any reason in particular?" he queried softly, stopping at the far end of the mantel and reaching a hand out toward her.

She winced. "It seems I have some trouble," she said, her voice shaking just a little. She hoped he wouldn't notice.

He lowered his hand, his expression becoming serious. "What trouble? Is it DuPres again? I'll kill him if he's touched you."

"Do you consider yourself a brave man, then, Your Grace?" she asked, unable to keep a sneer out of her voice at his pretended concern.

He tilted his head at her. "Brave? I don't consider myself a coward," he said after a moment.

"That's funny," she commented, watching him closely.

"What's funny?" he asked, confusion showing briefly on his face. Again he came toward her, and she circled around the back of the couch, keeping it between them. She held the pistol concealed behind her back, and it felt heavy and awkward in her hand.

"I consider you a coward," she spat out, unable to remain cool in the face of his obtuseness. "A coward and a liar and a villain."

"What are you up to, Kate?" he murmured, his expression going darker. "I told you it wasn't wise to bait me when we're alone together. Especially with you looking this attractive." He paused for a moment, looking at her. "You're not in trouble, are you?"

"No, I'm not," she responded. "But you are." She lifted the pistol in the air.

"Good God!" he exclaimed, a look of complete astonishment on his face. "What are you—"

"You are the greatest coward in the world," she continued.

His expression became even more confused. "Excuse my language," he grated out, "but what the hell are you talking about?"

"Only a great coward like you would pay his attentions

to a woman for the purpose of cheating her out of her inheritance."

"Cheat—" He abruptly shut his mouth and stared hard at her, then began to swear softly. "Crestley Hall. I should have realized. Damn Neville."

"No. Damn you, sir," she retorted, fighting to hold the shaking gun steady. "I won't let you steal my home away from me."

He took a step closer, and she leveled the pistol at his chest. "Katherine, you don't know the whole story. Believe me, I would not do this to you. Call Neville. He can explain."

"No."

He paused again, a cynical expression coming into his eyes as he looked down at the pistol. "What are you going to tell them, that I was trying to ravish you?"

She nodded, taking another step away from him as a grim smile came onto his face. "Don't smile," she hissed angrily. "I mean to do this."

"I have never doubted your resolve," he replied. "I only find it ironic that after everything I have done I am about to be sent to Jericho for something of which I am innocent."

"You are not innocent. And I am not one of those simpering chits who sighs at your absurd compliments and your roses and thinks you mean them. You didn't fool me for a moment."

This time his smile was genuinely amused. "But I did mean them," he said softly, eyeing the pistol as it wavered in her hand.

"You never did," she replied, steadying the heavy weapon with effort.

"Then what do you want of me? I am clearly at your mercy," he noted, far too calmly for her liking.

This was becoming somewhat confusing. "I want you to stop your purchase of Crestley Hall," she ordered.

"If I do, someone else will get it," he answered promptly.

"No, they won't," she retorted, tossing her head defiantly. "Crestley is mine."

"Excuse me, but have you considered that if I were wooing you for the sole purpose of stealing Crestley, all I would have to do is to convince you to marry me? As your husband it would come to me anyway, and at a considerably cheaper price."

She hadn't considered that. "It is because you mean never to marry," she declared. "Lord Neville told me so."

"That's two I owe him," Nicholas murmured.

"And because you don't care for me. It was only a ruse."

"Even if I gave my word to you, how do you know you can trust me?" he asked. "You have said I'm a liar and a coward."

"I suppose I shall have to trust you on that count," Katherine responded hesitantly, wondering when he had taken control of the proceedings.

"No," he said, shaking his head, his lips pursed thoughtfully. "If you refuse to believe that I can prove my innocence, I think you shall have to kill me."

"You are a villain!" she protested, wanting with all her heart to believe him and knowing that she couldn't. "I shall do it, you know."

"Do you really want to kill me?" he asked, his voice softer.

"No," she answered truthfully, knowing that she had never had any intention of doing so. She had never expected him to call her bluff. "I mean, yes," she corrected herself, frowning.

He raised his hands away from his body. "Then kill me. I have no other defense."

Doubt began to pull at her. She wanted him to be telling the truth. When she had been angry the thought of revenging herself on him had filled her with a grim satisfaction, but now everything had changed again. If only her heart would stop aching so, and leave her be. She started to lower the weapon, then jumped as she heard her godfather in the hall, no doubt wondering where Sommesby had got to. Abruptly Nicholas launched himself at her over the back of the couch. She shrieked and jerked the pistol away, and it went off.

Nicholas lurched sideways as the front window shattered and the sharp report echoed out into the street. With a surprised look on his face he collapsed onto the floor.

Katherine dropped the smoking pistol as the drawing-room door burst open. She had done it, when she hadn't meant to.

"Kate? What's going on?" Lord Neville asked, striding into the room.

Katherine pointed shakily at the far side of the couch. "I've killed him," she stammered, swaying dizzily.

"Killed whom?" he snapped, stepping around the end table.

"Nicholas," she whispered. "I've killed Nicholas." Her knees buckled, and she would have fallen if Rawlins hadn't come up behind her and braced her under the arms.

Lord Neville knelt down on the floor and touched his fingers to the duke's neck, then sat back with a sigh of relief. "You haven't killed him," he said. "Just put a hole in his shoulder. What in God's name happened?"

He wasn't dead. Katherine closed her eyes, hearing nothing else. She hadn't killed him. "He's trying to steal Crestley from me," she managed to say after a moment, forgetting that she had made up another story in case of an emergency.

"Trying to ... Oh, no, Kate. No. He's been trying to save it for you."

"What?" she exclaimed, incredulous. Nicholas had been telling her the truth. "Why didn't you tell me?"

"Because I am a great fool," her godfather replied. "Rawlins, help me get him upstairs." He glanced toward the doorway, where Lady Alison stood in front of the servants craning their necks to see into the room. "Alice, send for a doctor."

The two men were able to carry Nicholas upstairs into

one of the guest bedchambers. Though she tried to follow, Kate was banned from the room. A very pale Lady Alison led her to the library, where she poured them each a brandy.

"I think we need this," her godmother said, taking a swallow and choking a little. "Now, please, Kate, tell me what in the world possessed you to shoot Nick," she asked as she took a seat opposite Katherine.

"I never meant to shoot him," Kate protested. "Mr. Hodges gave me—" She paused at the confused look on her godmother's face. "I hired Mr. Hodges to look into Crestley Hall. He came by this morning to tell me that Nicholas was purchasing the deed. I thought . . . I thought that he had been so pleasant because he didn't want me to suspect that he was stealing it away from me."

Lady Alison groaned and sat back. "Oh, dear. We knew you had a stubborn streak, but my goodness, Kate, shooting the Duke of Sommesby?"

"I told you, it was an accident."

"I said from the beginning that we should have let you know what was going on," Lady Alison said, disgust in her voice.

"What is going on, then?"

"Neville had a suspicion that your uncle would try to sell Crestley, very quietly. He knew that he couldn't become involved because Simon would have recognized the Hampton name and suspected a trap, so he asked Nick to purchase it for him, no questions asked."

"And the duke agreed to that?" Katherine asked somewhat skeptically.

"Yes." Her godmother looked at her again for a long moment. "Until he realized that Crestley was yours and that you had no idea what we were planning. He made Neville promise to tell you, which he did try to do, unsuccessfully, yesterday morning."

Nicholas had been telling the truth. He hadn't played her along, at least not for the purpose of stealing Crestley. "Why didn't you tell me?" she wailed.

"Oh, my dear, we knew you were determined to handle this on your own. We were concerned that if you knew Crestley was being put up for sale, you might do something rash."

"Such as shoot someone?" she asked with a shudder.

The library door opened, and Lord Neville entered. Katherine found herself on her feet, facing him. "Is he all right?" she asked, her voice breaking.

Her godfather crossed the room to pour himself a stiff drink. "The ball went clean through. He's lost some blood, but the doctor says he'll live." He knocked back the brandy, then looked over at Kate, who was twisting her hands in front of her green muslin skirt. "He's asked to see you."

Before he could say anything further Katherine was out the door and running up the stairs. Outside the room she paused, abruptly nervous. Then she took a deep breath and knocked. The doctor, a short, portly man with red cheeks, opened the door.

"I've given him laudanum," he informed her. "Don't tax him overly much."

"Too late for that," an irritated voice said from the bed.

12

"You may go, Doctor," Nicholas said as Katherine hesitantly entered. "And thank you."

The doctor nodded. "I'll come by this afternoon to change your bandages, Your Grace," he responded, exiting the bedchamber with a bow.

Katherine stared at Nicholas from across the room, her blue eyes wide and her face white. He knew he must look about the same, for even with the laudanum his shoulder and arm throbbed. "Come over here," he finally commanded when she made no move to approach.

It was a measure of how upset she was that she did as he said. "How do you feel?" she asked in a small voice.

"How am I supposed to feel?" he retorted. "You shot me."

Color appeared in her cheeks again. "It was your fault," she returned. "I wasn't going to shoot you at all, and then you attacked me."

"My fault?" he retorted. "You summon me to meet with you, lie to me, threaten my life, and shoot me, and it's my fault?"

She began crying. "I thought you were trying to steal Crestley from me," she said, sobbing, and wringing her slim hands in the folds of her skirt. "I feel so awful. I might have killed you."

"Not with your aim," he muttered, and held out his hand. He hadn't expected her to cry, and it curiously touched him. Women had attempted to use tears on him before, and, when he had refused to react, labeled him hardhearted or cruel. She came forward and took his hand in her own, and he squeezed her fingers. "Don't cry, Kate," he murmured.

"I'm not crying," she answered, sniffling. "I'm only tired."

"Yes, I would imagine you are," he answered dryly, the laudanum beginning to make him feel lethargic. "You've been quite busy this morning." He and Neville had spoken, rather harshly, a few moments earlier, and after what Katherine must have discovered, he was surprised she hadn't really tried to kill him. "Have you been told about my part in these dealings?"

She nodded and wiped at her eyes. "I still want you to stop," she said, tightening her grip on his hand.

"Why?"

"Because I won't pay for my own property."

"I'm paying for it, remember?" he reminded her, his words slurring a little.

"I would be obligated to repay you," she responded.

Nicholas found that his eyes were shut, and he forced them open again to look up into her deep-blue ones. "You don't have to repay me," he answered slowly. "It would be my gift."

She shook her head. "I would be obligated to repay you," she repeated. "Are you truly that wealthy?" she asked curiously, cocking her head.

He chuckled, wincing as that jarred his shoulder. "Even wealthier than that."

"There must be another way to stop my uncle," she went on. "Please say you won't buy Crestley, and help me figure out something else," she said softly.

His eyes shut again at the silky sound of her voice. "All right," he murmured, and then was asleep.

* * *

When he awoke again the curtains had been pulled back, letting in the afternoon sun. Katherine stood by the bed arranging two roses, a white one with several petals missing and a very badly bent red one, in a small vase. "What happened to those poor things?" he asked sleepily.

"They were the best ones left after I dumped the bouquet you sent me into the chamber pot," she explained, her eyes twinkling. "I'll find you some better ones out in the garden."

"Into the chamber pot?" he echoed, trying to force the cobwebs out of his brain.

"I was very angry this morning," she reminded him. She seated herself in the chair someone had placed by the bed.

"You'd think I'd be used to having people angry at me by now," he muttered, mostly to himself. The anger of most people didn't concern him at all, but the hurt and fury in her eyes that morning had been alarming and disturbing.

"Do that many people dislike you?" she asked, raising an eyebrow.

"Tally all of my personal, business, and political acquaintances, and yes, that many people dislike me." And she wasn't the first person to try to kill him, though he preferred not to go into that.

"Do you like being disliked?" she asked after a moment.

"Like it?" he repeated, not expecting the question. "I suppose I really hadn't thought that much about it."

Katherine looked away toward the window. "I would find it very lonely, I think," she said quietly.

He looked at her profile in the sunlight, barely resisting the urge to finger the dark curls of her hair that hung over one shoulder, then chuckled. "It's not as though everyone in England despises me, you know. I'm not all that terrible. Occasionally I even do something pleasant." It occurred to him that a few short weeks ago he never would have been able to confess that perhaps he did have a good side. Perhaps no one before Katherine had ever tried to find it.

Her lips quirked as she looked back at him. "Occasionally. Maybe."

"Nicky," His mother's voice came from the doorway.

He turned his head. "It's all right, Mama, don't send for Cousin Julius in Paris yet. I believe I still have a few breaths left in my body."

"I'm certain Julius will be disappointed to hear that," Julia Varon replied, the tense lines in her face easing. She sent a sharp glance at Katherine and him, and Nicholas wondered how much she knew, or had guessed. His mother missed very little.

Katherine stood. "I shall leave you to talk," she said, smiling at his mother. She slipped out of the room before he could protest.

The Dowager Duchess took Katherine's vacated seat. "We have put out the story that you were here on business. As you rose to get a glass of brandy you were shot through the window."

"The window? Inventing an assassin is a bit much, don't you think?" He shifted uncomfortably, already tired of lying flat on his back. "Kate's not the best shot, but she did hit me, after all."

"Mon dieu, do not tease. You might have been killed," she reprimanded sternly. She leaned forward and tapped him on his good shoulder with one finger. "And you have someone else's reputation to consider this time."

He nodded. "You're right."

"Did she really shoot you, *mon fils?"* Julia asked, her gray eyes twinkling.

"Yes, by God, though she didn't mean to. I was trying to disarm her, and she squeezed the trigger. I should have known better."

Julia Varon sat back, looking at him for a long time. "You love her, yes?" she asked finally.

Nicholas looked at the two pitiful roses dying in their vase and grinned. "Yes." He had realized it after his return from the picnic. He had sat in his study planning battle strategies for their next encounter, and abruptly realized that he had already lost the war. Or perhaps he had won. Katherine had unsettled him so much at their first encounter that he had likely been trying to make her fall in love with him ever since, out of revenge. Instead, he had fallen for her.

His mother returned his smile. "I am so happy for you, *mon enfant,*" she responded. "I like her very much."

"Don't be happy for me yet," he commented. "I still have a long way to go before I can convince Katherine that I'm not bamming her. I have enough pride left that I don't intend to declare myself to her and then have her laugh at me."

"You do mean to offer for her, then?" Julia asked, clearly delighted.

"When I can be certain she'll say yes. She's a bit ... unpredictable."

"Nicholas," the duchess said unsympathetically, "sometimes you must take a chance. Love is never predictable. That is why it is so special."

"End of lecture?" he said testily. He would handle Katherine—not that he yet had a clue how to manage it.

"End of lecture," Julia agreed with a faint smile.

Nicholas's valet finally arrived with appropriate wardrobe and necessities, and the next morning he dressed in a loose-fitting house jacket and sat up in the chair for a while. The wound wasn't that bad, and he likely could have made it back to Varon House, but he had little inclination to do so as long as he had an excuse to remain under the Hamptons' roof for another day or two.

He and Neville had been discussing alternatives to his plan to purchase Crestley, with little success, when Katherine's knock sounded at the door. "Come in," he called.

She had donned a pale-yellow sprig muslin dress, and her black hair was swept back in a long tail. In her hands she carried a well-wrapped package and a vase of garden flowers, which she placed next to the window. She was the first female ever to bring him flowers, he realized with a grin.

"Good morning." She smiled, leaning over to kiss Neville on the cheek. "Have you considered a solicitor?" she asked, straightening to look at the duke. "Mr. Hodges offered his services to me."

Nicholas shook his head, for he and Neville had just been debating that. "I'm not convinced that would be a wise idea."

"The property is hers, Nick."

"Yes, but Simon Ralston is the younger sibling of the owner of the estate, and a male. If this goes to court he has a chance of wresting Crestley from Katherine legally, even if it isn't entailed." Nicholas leaned forward stiffly. "Besides, this could easily be tangled up in the courts for years, leaving Ralston on the property as the proprietor until settlement."

"No," Kate said. "I won't have that."

"An estate is a difficult thing to steal, or I would suggest we try that," he said dryly. "The easiest thing would be to do as we planned and let me simply buy it and give you the deed."

"Nicholas, I already told you, I have no—"

He waved his hand at her. "I know. You have no intention of paying for your own property. The problem, dear Kate, is that by the time you inherit it, there may be nothing left."

"There will be if he doesn't sell it to anyone," she retorted.

Out of the corner of his eye Nicholas noted that Clarey had risen and left the room. Apparently the baron still considered him too weak to be a threat to Kate's virtue. "If he doesn't sell to me, he'll sell to someone else. I've already had to outbid five other parties to get this far."

"Other parties," she repeated slowly. "I'd forgotten about that."

"Did you forget that one of them is Francis DuPres?" At

her stricken look he abruptly wished that he had remained silent.

"I didn't forget that. And I won't have him setting foot in Crestley Hall," she spat out, rising and striding about the room in a rather unladylike manner. "He will not buy his precious respectability with my home. I won't allow it."

"Well," Nicholas said slowly, following her with his eyes and rubbing his suddenly sweaty palms against his thighs, "there is one other way you could keep Crestley Hall safe."

She returned to his side. "What is it?" she asked hopefully.

He started to answer, then found that he couldn't do it. Not that anyone would believe it, but the Black Duke was terrified that the spitfire schoolroom chit gazing expectantly at him would turn him down. He cleared his throat. "We just haven't thought of it yet," he replied, improvising.

"Really, Nicholas," she said disgustedly. "That's no help."

"What's in the package?" he asked, to change the subject. He pointed at the object she had left sitting by the flowers.

She walked over to retrieve it. "I forgot. It came for you this morning, from your mother."

"Will you open it?" he asked, wondering with some trepidation what it might be. He wouldn't have put much past Julia Varon.

"It's one of the quartos," Katherine exclaimed after a moment as she lifted it out of the heavy, protective paper.

"I should have realized that I need merely get shot to have her send me one," he remarked, and Katherine laughed at him. "Which is it? Perhaps we could read it together."

"I would like that," she said, glancing down at it. Abruptly the stubborn expression that he was beginning to know, came into her face.

"Which one is it?" he asked again, intrigued.

"I'm not going to tell you," she said flatly.

"No? Then show me," he suggested.

She shook her head. "No."

"Katherine," he warned, "give it to me."

"It's *The Taming of the Shrew,*" she finally answered, glaring at him.

Nicholas gave a shout of laughter. So she saw similarities between herself and the shrewish Kate, did she? Katherine rose, heading for the door. "Katherine, wait," he pleaded.

"I am no longer speaking to you," she said over her shoulder.

"I've just started rereading the comedies in their original order. *The Shrew* is next. That's all there is to it." She continued toward the door, her chin in the air. "Katherine, I swear it," he said, chuckling.

"I shall consider returning later, Your Grace," she said haughtily, and exited the room, leaving him behind to resume his laughter.

13

U sed as the servants at Hampton House were to entertaining high-ranking members of the *ton,* the presence of the Duke of Sommesby had whipped them into
something of a frenzy. Even the already overdignified
Rawlins seemed to stand straighter and loom taller with
the Black Duke present.

Katherine found it rather amusing once she was certain
Nicholas would be all right. She had been more worried
than she could say, and if she hadn't thought that he would
laugh at her, she would have told him so. She had finally
agreed to read *The Shrew,* but only because he'd teased her
unmercifully and told her she was cowhearted.

On the morning of the third day of his stay at Hampton
House she went into the garden to pick more flowers for
the vase in his chamber. It was silly, she knew, but they
gave her an excuse to visit him.

"Katherine?"

She jumped, and turned around. Nicholas, jacketless and
looking handsome and a bit pale in buckskin breeches and
a black waistcoat, stood leaning against the wall of the
house. Katherine blushed, wondering how long he had
been watching her. "Good morning."

"Good morning." When he reached her side he leaned
over and sniffed the flowers bunched in her hand, and it

was only with a conscious effort that she resisted running her fingers through his dark hair. "For me?" he asked, raising his head to look at her.

She nodded, abruptly fascinated by the deep-emerald flecks in his gray eyes. "You and the duchess have such pretty eyes," she said, wishing his would keep looking at her in that amused, affectionate way forever.

"My father used to say that the Varon family's greatest wealth lay in the emerald of my mother's eyes," he murmured, then reached out to touch Katherine's cheek. "Though I find my favorite gem to be the sapphire of yours."

"Oh, my," Kate whispered, then cleared her throat and turned away. "I wanted to tell you, we'll have to delay finishing the play until tomorrow. I'm going riding with Thomas and the others today."

"You see Thomas quite a bit, don't you?" he asked coolly, his eyes on the garden.

"He's very nice to me," she replied, watching his face and wondering what he was thinking.

"I'm nice," he responded, his eyes glinting as he looked back at her.

"I thought we had decided that you were irritating, selfish, and provoking," she returned with a grin.

"Ah," he said, raising an eyebrow, "you have used those same epithets on me before."

"You continue to earn them," she pointed out.

"You put me to the blush, m'dear," he drawled, walking over to the stone bench by the path and seating himself. He fiddled with his watch fob for a moment, then looked up at her. "I'm going home this afternoon," he said. "If I stay any longer people will begin to talk, if they haven't begun already."

She looked away to hide her sudden keen disappointment that he was leaving. "Can you ride?"

"I believe I will manage."

"I'm sorry I shot you," she apologized for the fiftieth time, sitting beside him.

He grinned. "We both know it was my fault." He touched her sleeve. "And I've never been wounded by a more attractive assassin."

She wasn't certain whether that was a compliment or not, and frowned. "Would it have hurt more if I'd been ugly?" she countered.

"Infinitely," he replied. His hand drifted down her arm to her wrist, and she shivered at the feathery-light touch. He turned her hand to caress her palm, then twined his fingers with hers and tugged her closer.

"You think to win the argument this way, then?" she commented, finding that her voice was shaking.

"Mm-hm." He raised her chin with his fingertips and kissed her.

He was cheating again, but she decided that was all right. Nicholas captured her other hand and placed both of her arms up around his neck before he let his palms slide slowly down her body to her waist.

"Kate?"

Her entire body tingling, she pulled away and shot to her feet as Thomas came around the corner. The viscount came to an abrupt stop as he saw them. Nicholas remained seated, and though she didn't remember having dropped them, the flowers she had picked were strewn across the bench and on the ground.

"Nick." The viscount spoke stiffly, his easy expression darkening. "Glad to see you're all right."

"Thank you, Thomas," Nicholas returned coolly.

Katherine looked back and forth at the two of them for a moment, feeling the tension there, and then smoothed at her skirts. "Thomas, come inside," she said, and both gazes shifted to her, angry pale-blue eyes and enigmatic dark-gray ones. "I need to get my hat and gloves, and then we can go."

"Of course, Kate." The viscount offered her his arm. She took it, and they headed back toward the house.

"Katherine."

She turned her head. Nicholas had picked up one of the

discarded flowers and tucked it into a buttonhole of his waistcoat. *"Au revoir,"* he said, his accent impeccable.

"Can you make it inside on your own?" she asked, stopping.

"I believe so. If not, I assume someone will come looking for me eventually."

She nodded, chuckling, and allowed Thomas to lead her inside. He waited at the foot of the stairs while she hurried up to get her things. The groom had already saddled Winter, and in only a few moments they were on their way to Hyde Park. With Nicholas hurt, she and the Hamptons had remained housebound, and this was the first time she had been out in several days.

"Kate, I know I have no claim on you and it is therefore not my place to speak, but if Nick has overstepped his bounds I beg that you will let me see to it that he ceases bothering you." The viscount's voice was deeply serious, and she was torn between amusement at his concern and annoyance at his presumption.

"No one has overstepped anything," she replied, nodding as they passed an acquaintance whose name she could not at that moment recall.

"But I saw—"

"No one has overstepped anything," she repeated firmly, and though he blustered for a moment, he didn't press her further.

He sulked for the rest of the afternoon, however, which had the result of making her testy and bringing Althaea close to tears. For the first time she noted how closely the girl observed the viscount, and saw how hard she tried to raise his spirits, to no avail. Kate knew that Louisa and Reg were in love, but she hadn't realized Althaea had a *tendre* for Thomas Elder. Evidently the viscount hadn't realized it either, for he was so concerned with being jealous of the Black Duke's erratic attentions to her that he barely noticed the brown-eyed beauty.

On the return home he began pestering her again, and she decided she had had enough. "Thomas, stop it."

"I only have your best interests in mind," he protested.

"I thought you and Sommesby were friends," she responded.

"We are," he agreed. "It's just that . . . that I care for you, and I doubt he has your best interests in mind. He is infamous for breaking hearts."

"I am aware of his reputation," she informed him with a frown, "and I can take care of myself."

"But you can't, Kate. People are already beginning to talk, to wonder if you are the Black Duke's latest."

She imagined that question to be on his mind as well. She couldn't answer it, because she had no idea herself. "I don't care what people think," she declared.

"You should."

"You were a great deal more fun before you became so stiff," she said with a sniff.

"I am not stiff," he protested, his voice rising an indignant octave.

"Yes, you are, and I shan't ride with you any longer. Go home, Thomas."

"Not until I've seen you back to Hampton House," he replied, still acting entirely too stiff for her taste. Perhaps she had spent too much time in Nicholas's lax company.

"Nonsense. It's only a street away. Go home."

"Only if you say you're not angry at me," he said, giving in a little.

"I'm not angry at you. And I shall consider what you have said," she added, though for that moment she had no intention of doing anything about it. Not if it meant she couldn't see Nicholas any longer.

"All right, then. May I call on you for tea tomorrow?"

"Of course," she replied.

He inclined his head and then pulled Orpheus around to leave her to ride on by herself. She rode Winter to the stable, and William, the groom, helped her dismount. As she walked to the house she pulled off her hat, tired of the way the pins stuck into her scalp, and wondered if Nicholas had returned to Varon House already or whether they had time to finish Act Four of *The Shrew*. Abruptly someone grabbed her from behind.

Before she could protest, a dirty hand was placed over her mouth. Terrified, she kicked out backward and was rewarded by a grunt and an oath, and then she was pulled off balance, and someone grabbed her legs. Both men were dirty-looking and dressed in rough homespun, and she was certain that she had never seen them before.

Although Kate fought them all the way, the men dragged her around to the back of the house, where the second one produced a stout rope, bound her legs, and tied her hands behind her back. The men gagged her, and then a smelly cloth sack was pulled over her head, so that she couldn't see.

She was lifted again, and after a very short time her hip bumped cruelly against something and she was dumped on the ground. Not the ground, she realized as it began to move. She was in some sort of coach. Panicking, she flailed about again, and was rewarded by a rough kick in the leg.

"Stop your fighting, missy, or you'll get worse than that," a gruff voice said, and she was shoved over on her side with the toe of a boot.

She lay still, wondering what was happening, where she was being taken. Her panicked thoughts went to Nicholas, and she hoped with all her heart that wherever he was he would know that she desperately needed help.

Nicholas was dozing before the fire in his library when a rapid pounding sounded at the front door. His shoulder ached despite the two glasses of brandy he had consumed after supper, and he had been loath to rise and make his way upstairs to his bedchamber. Sleepily he looked at the clock on the mantel. It was just past eight, so his visitor was likely one of his cronies, wondering why he had ceased attending his clubs. He hoped Grimsby would get rid of whoever it was, so he wouldn't have to explain that a madcap schoolroom chit had him so distracted he seemed unable to win a game of jackstraws or bilbo-catch, much less faro.

The library door was flung open, and he started and turned to view his uninvited guest. "Neville?" he exclaimed, for the Baron of Clarey was the last person he would have expected.

"Is she here?" Neville asked, looking frantically about the room. "By God, if she is, you've made an enemy of me!"

Grimsby had followed Neville into the room, and with a jerk of his head Nicholas motioned him out. More than used to odd goings-on at the Black Duke's residence, the butler complied and shut the door behind him. "What the devil are you talking about?" he asked once they were alone. Neville looked more than half in a panic, which was unusual enough in itself, and the baron's words had started a queer, uneasy feeling in the pit of his stomach.

"Is she here? Is Kate here? Your damned closemouthed butler wouldn't say whether you were entertaining anyone or not!"

"Why in the world would Katherine be here?" Nicholas asked, sitting up a little straighter and ignoring the fact that until several weeks ago it wouldn't have been unusual at all for him to be entertaining a woman at home.

"Please, Nick, just answer me," Neville pleaded, continuing to pace around the room. "I'll forgive you. Just tell me she's here."

"She's not here," Nicholas said flatly, the feeling of uneasiness in his stomach changing to one of dread. "Tell me what's happened."

"She's gone."

Nicholas stood. "What do you mean, 'She's gone'? Explain yourself, man."

"She went riding with Sheresford and the Hillarys, rode back on her own, and brought her mare to the stables. She never came back inside." Neville held out a crumpled lump of mauve felt. "We found her hat halfway between the stables and the house."

"Let me see it," Nicholas ordered.

Neville sat heavily in one of the chairs. "Nick," he whispered, "someone's taken Kate."

Nicholas clutched Katherine's riding hat in his hands. He was angry, quite possibly more than he'd ever been in his life. Someone had taken his Katherine, and someone was going to pay. And pay dearly. "You said she rode back on her own," he murmured. "Where the hell was Sheresford?"

"I went to Thomas's first. They apparently had something of a disagreement, and she refused to ride further with him. He said they were only a street or so from home."

"The fool," Nicholas spat out.

"He's gone to the Hillarys' and to the Dremonds' to see if Kate's there. He's the one who suggested she might be here." Neville's face was drawn and gray, and if Nicholas had needed any proof that the Hamptons cared deeply for their goddaughter, he saw it in the Baron of Clarey's worried countenance.

"And you naturally thought that might be so," he said with a sneer.

"You've made your own reputation," Neville retorted, then stood, blanching. "I'm sorry. I'm half out of my mind. If anything happens to her . . ."

"Nothing is going to happen to her," Nicholas snapped, refusing to believe otherwise. "If she's been kidnapped, it must be for some purpose."

"Kate has done nothing . . . except to be seen with you."

"I know." If Katherine had been taken because of him, because of something he had done, he would never forgive himself. Other than Josette Bettreaux and her young conspirator, there had been nothing blatant of late. And Josette, as far as he knew, was still in Paris nursing her wounds. He straightened, cursing. There was one other possibility, something that Kate had most definitely been involved in. "Francis DuPres," he said.

"DuPres?" Clarey echoed. "I know he's an annoyance, but kidnapping?"

A knock came at the library door. "Not now, Grimsby!" he said with a growl.

"It's Gladstone, Your Grace," came his secretary's muffled voice.

"Not now, Glad—" He stopped abruptly, another horrifying thought jolting into his mind. He strode over to yank open the door. "Get in here."

Gladstone complied, nodding at the baron as he entered. "With your recent incapacitation I thought you might have forgotten our schedule regarding"—Gladstone paused to glance at Neville—"regarding that property up north," he continued, "so I thought to stop by and remind you."

Nicholas waved an arm at him, thinking madly. "Never mind the secrets," he said. "The Baron knows all about it."

"Oh, splendid," Gladstone said, and took a seat, opening his case in his lap. "Well, then—"

"Quiet," Nicholas interrupted before his secretary could get started. "Was Mr. Smith aware that the heir would have to sign the Crestley Hall deed over to make the transfer legal?"

"Oh, God," Neville moaned, sinking back into his chair and covering his face with his hands.

"Why, yes, Your Grace. In fact, he brought it up before I could remind him of the fact. He informed me that there would be no problem. And you pointed out several days ago that he would likely handle that little difficulty himself."

It was Nicholas's turn to groan. When he had so callously suggested that getting the heir to sign the deed was not his problem, he had had no idea that the "youth" they had been referring to was Katherine Ralston.

"What have I done?" Neville whispered.

"You thought you were acting in her best interests," Nicholas replied. Neville was distressed enough as it was. "Don't fault yourself for that."

"Your Grace, might I inquire as to what is going on?" Gladstone asked, looking up curiously.

Nicholas nodded. "The heir to Crestley is Neville's god-daughter, and we believe that she has been kidnapped by her uncle, our Mr. Smith." Gladstone had known the intimate details of the Duke of Sommesby's finances for years, and Nicholas saw no reason not to trust him with this.

"I see the complication," Gladstone commented, frowning.

"Is everything prepared for my trip to Crestley?" Nicholas asked him.

"Yes. I did as you instructed, and the proper amount of currency has been collected and is being held until Thursday, when we were to depart."

Nicholas had forgotten that the purchase was to be made with cash. That would make things easier. "Can you get the money tonight?"

"I would imagine that could be accomplished, Your Grace," Gladstone replied, his tone indicating that the request might have been substantially more difficult to grant if it hadn't been the Duke of Sommesby who was making it.

"Good." Nicholas returned to the door and opened it. "Grimsby, have Jack hitch up the coach immediately!" he bellowed, and shut the door again.

"Nick, you can't travel all the way to Crestley with your shoulder like that," Neville protested.

Clarey was likely right, but it didn't matter. This needed to be done. "Be back here in an hour, Gladstone. The hell with Mr. Smith's waiting period. I want that deed, and I want it now."

"I'm going with you," Neville said firmly, rising again.

Nicholas shook his head. "No. If Ralston sees you, he might panic. There would be questions if another Ralston were to die suddenly, but if he can't sell Crestley off, he might be tempted to get it through inheritance."

The older man sagged. Neville must blame himself for

all this, Nicholas knew, and now there was nothing the baron could do to set it right. "You and Alison start out at about noon tomorrow," he suggested. "It's likely too late, but if there is anything that can be done to save Katherine's reputation, I'm most certainly not the one to do it."

Neville straightened again, nodding. "I'll put out word to her friends that her uncle has taken ill. We'll leave it at that for now." He started toward the door, then stopped and looked back. "Find her, Nick."

"I will, Neville. I swear it."

14

After two days of being shoved and jostled about, Katherine finally realized where she was being taken. The sounds outside the coach became increasingly familiar, and as she recognized the bleat of Georgie Gurstin's sheep in the pasture and the ringing bell in the steeple of the All Souls' Church, she even relaxed a little. They were bringing her home.

The coach lurched to a stop, and she was roughly jerked upright. Her arms and legs were numb, and she stifled a groan as she stumbled. She was handed down to the ground and stumbled again, this time falling and banging her shoulder.

"Pick her up and bring her into the house," said her uncle's voice.

She was yanked upright once more, and then thrown over someone's shoulder like a sack of greens. She was dumped into a chair upstairs, and a moment later heard the rattle of chains. Something clamped painfully around her ankle, and then the sack was yanked off her head.

She was in her old bedchamber. The two men stood off to one side, smirking at her, while her uncle stood before her with his arms crossed. "Welcome back to Crestley, Kate," he said smugly, and she longed to slap him. "Untie her."

They did as he bid, slitting the ropes that bound her arms. A metal band had been locked around her left ankle, and a chain trailed from it to the heavy bed frame. Her riding dress was ripped and soiled, its original mauve color barely distinguishable. Simon Ralston stepped forward and pulled her gag down.

"You blackguard," she spat out.

He ignored her, motioning the men out of the room and turning away. At the doorway he stopped and turned back. "There is food and water on the dressing table. As you can see, it is impossible for you to leave the room." He gestured at the chain.

Before she could manage a reply he was gone, shutting the door behind him and locking it. Her hands began to throb painfully, and tears she hadn't realized she was crying trickled down her face. Beyond exhaustion, she stumbled to the bed wondering where Nicholas was, and if he would come after her.

A full day passed before she saw Uncle Simon again. A coach rumbled up the drive, but the chain didn't reach far enough for her to be able to look out the window and see what was happening. Half an hour later the key turned in the lock. Her uncle strode in, slamming the door behind him. His face was pale, and he looked highly agitated.

"You listen to me, Kate. You clean yourself up, fix your hair, and put on a clean dress." He crossed the room and yanked open her wardrobe, pawing through the few gowns that remained. He pulled out her least favorite, a brown muslin with long sleeves and a high neck that had always made her feel like a goose. "This one," he said, throwing it on the bed.

"I can't change with this on," she protested, pointing at the chain. She had already tried removing it, with no success.

He swore at her. "All right," he snapped, pushing her back into the chair, "but I warn you, if you try anything—*anything*—it'll be the last trick you pull." He knelt and unlocked the band, then stood and turned away. "I'll be back in a few minutes. You be ready."

Because she had no choice, she did as he told her. Her hair had been pulled, stepped on, and slept on for three days, but she brushed it out as best she could and pulled it into a long tail down her back. She used the glass of tepid water and a corner of her riding habit to clean off her face. When she pulled on the dress she saw why he had picked it. The long sleeves covered most of the bruises on her wrists.

There was little else she could do, and she was ready when he returned. "You'll do," he muttered. "Get up. You play the good girl when we get downstairs, and do exactly as you're told." He pulled her toward the door. "Understand?"

"Yes," she answered shortly, wincing as he wrenched her tender shoulder.

She went down the stairs slowly, hanging onto the rail, for she was stiff and shaky and didn't want to fall. Simon Ralston guided her to her father's old office and shoved open the door. He gripped her arm tightly enough to bruise it and pulled her into the room. She stumbled a little and, frightened and furious, kept her eyes on the floor.

"Mr. Gladstone," her uncle began in an unctuous voice, "Your Grace, my niece, Kate Ralston. Kate, His Grace, The Duke of Sommesby."

Nicholas stood as Katherine lifted her eyes with a visible start. It was only a decade of experience at displaying aloofness that kept him from going to her and pulling her trembling body into his arms. Her face was white, her dark-blue eyes enormous with shock and fatigue as she stared at him.

"Good morning, Miss Ralston," he drawled. "I believe we were introduced once at Almack's, were we not?" he continued, playing the Black Duke to the hilt and hoping she would realize what he was doing.

The look in her eyes sharpened. "I believe it was at the Hillary ball, Your Grace," she replied in a tired voice.

She understood. Just in time Nicholas stopped himself from smiling at her. Ralston pushed her toward the nearest chair, and she reached out to hold onto the back to steady herself. As she did so, Nicholas got a glimpse of her wrist, and couldn't restrain his angry hiss at the sight of the bruised flesh.

Ralston looked at him sharply, and Nick reached up to rub his shoulder and rudely seated himself before Katherine. "You may have heard," he drawled. "Had something of a firearms accident recently."

With a quick glance at him Katherine seated herself, and her uncle and Gladstone followed suit. At Nicholas's nod Gladstone pulled several heavy pieces of paper out of his case and laid them on the table. "You have the deed, Mr. Smith . . . ah . . . Ralston?" Gladstone questioned.

Nicholas had had a difficult time not sneering as Ralston explained his reason for using a false name. As he told it, he was worried that his family's monetary situation would reflect badly on his niece, and so he had taken this extra precaution to keep the Ralston name from being bandied about London. His concern for his family name hadn't kept him from kidnapping Kate, but Nicholas refrained for the moment from pointing that out.

"I have the deed," Ralston said, patting a thick envelope in front of him. "Do you have the money?"

"Such vulgarity, Mr. Ralston," Nicholas said reprovingly, examining his fingernails.

"I am only concerned for my niece's future, Your Grace," Ralston replied.

"Of course. We all are," Nicholas agreed, glancing over at Katherine and trying not to put any additional meaning into the words.

"We have the agreed-on amount, in currency, as you requested," Gladstone said, looking through his case again and glancing up briefly.

"Splendid. Let's get on with it, then, shall we?" Simon

Ralston pulled his chair forward and craned his neck at the papers Gladstone had produced, looking to Nicholas like some sort of vulture.

"With Your Grace's permission?" his secretary requested.

Nicholas nodded regally, and Gladstone slid the papers over to Ralston. "You have there four copies of the agreement signing over the deed. His Grace has already signed them as recipient of the deed. First you must sign them as guardian, and then Miss Ralston shall sign them as heir."

Ralston nodded impatiently, grabbed the pen from the desk, and he dipped it in ink. He scrawled his signature on all four pieces of paper, then slid them over to Katherine. "Sign them, Kate," he said.

Nicholas heard the threat in his unctuous tone and had to restrain a growl as Katherine shook her head. She had balked at the idea all along, and she was stubborn as the tide, but Nicholas had to make her understand that she needed to sign the papers so he could proceed with the plan he and Gladstone had hastily concocted on the way north.

"Please, Miss Ralston," he drawled, leaning forward and flicking his long fingers carelessly at the papers, "sign these things so we may conclude this odious business."

She glanced up at him, and he held her gaze for a long moment. Then, her hand shaking, she picked up the pen and dipped it in the well. After a long hesitation she signed each one of the papers and then dropped the pen back onto the table.

"Now the money," Ralston snarled as Gladstone took the papers back and examined them.

"First things first, Mr. Ralston," the secretary demurred. "The deed, if you please. You understand, I must be absolutely certain that it is the original," he continued, looking at it closely, "with nothing added or removed that could possibly call the legality of the document into question." Finally he nodded and handed it over to his employer. "Everything seems in order, Your Grace."

"Very well," Nicholas said, and Gladstone lifted the

heavy case he had been guarding with his life since their departure from London. Carrying a hundred thousand pounds about was enough to make even Nicholas edgy.

Gladstone set the valise on the table in front of Katherine, evading Ralston's grab. "Here you are, Miss Ralston," he said. "Payment in full for Crestley Hall."

Ralston again reached for it, but Nicholas negligently raised a hand. "You know, Ralston," he drawled, "you really should take care to dress your niece in clothing more befitting her station."

"Beg pardon?" Ralston muttered, glancing up at him.

"I said I seem to recall your niece dressed more fashionably in London."

Ralston, still eyeing the money case, cleared his throat. "Well, we live more simply in the country, Your Grace," he explained absently.

"Ah," Nicholas said noncommittally, privately seething. "I see. Now that I think of it, though, I was particularly fond of the riding habit she wore several mornings ago in the garden at Hampton House. Do you recall the one I mean, Katherine?"

Ralston's face went white, and he started to rise. Nicholas reached into his coat pocket and produced a pistol, which he laid on the table in front of him.

"Yes, Nicholas, I remember the one you refer to," Katherine answered. Her eyes glinted when she raised her head to look at him.

"Nicho—" Her uncle stopped short, staring at his niece. "What is going on here?"

"Do you know that you could be sent up to Newgate for life for kidnapping and theft of property?" Nicholas asked casually, leaning forward and dropping the affected drawl from his voice. "Actually, though, with my influence I am certain I could arrange to have you hanged for it."

Ralston blanched. "I don't know what you're talking about," he stammered.

"Oh, I think you do," Nicholas murmured. He looked

over at Kate. "Do you have anything in mind for your uncle, my love, or may I see to this for you?"

She glared at Simon Ralston for a moment. "As long as you don't kill him and I never have to see him again, I don't care what you do," she said flatly.

Nicholas nodded. He reached into his coat again and produced a large roll of currency. He tossed it at Ralston, who caught it as it slapped against his chest. "That is one thousand pounds. I suggest you use it wisely, for you will receive nothing more. I also suggest that you use it to leave the country, perhaps for the colonies. The Americas are rumored to be a land of great opportunity."

"You can't make me leave," Ralston spat out. "I am Kate's guardian."

"And now you will be her guardian from across the Atlantic," Nicholas snapped. "Don't try me further, Ralston. As you may have heard, I have very little patience. If it were not for Katherine's request, I would kill you for what you've done to her." He shoved the pistol over to his secretary, who picked it up and aimed it at Ralston. "See that he gathers his things together. He will be leaving in one-quarter hour. Make certain he takes with him nothing belonging to this estate."

"With pleasure, Your Grace," Gladstone muttered, smiling grimly as he motioned Ralston to his feet.

The two men left the room, and Nicholas rose and made his way around the desk. "Katherine?" he said softly, taking the seat beside her.

She hurled herself against his chest, and he enfolded her in his arms. She sobbed brokenly against his neck, clinging to him tightly. "I knew you would come," she whispered, "I knew you would come."

"How could I not?" he replied, burying his face in her long black hair.

Finally she calmed a little and raised her tear-stained face to look at him. "So now Crestley is yours, after all."

He shook his head and handed her the deed. "Crestley

may be in my name, but it is yours, and always shall be. Consider me its . . . guardian angel."

She reached out and touched the valise. "If Crestley is still mine, then this money is still yours."

He shook his head, raising a finger to her lips when she began to protest. "We shall discuss that later."

He pulled her closer and stood, lifting her in his arms. Abruptly he deposited her back on the other chair, grimacing at her surprised look at such cavalier treatment. "Just a moment," he said, and walked to the window. "Jack, get in here!" he bellowed, and then returned to her. "I am truly sorry, and I intend to make up for my lack of chivalry at a later date, but I'm certain that if I attempt to carry you up to your bedchamber, I shall likely dump both of us on the stairs."

"Your wound!" she said with a gasp, reaching out to touch his sleeve.

"Damnably inconvenient," he acknowledged ruefully.

"I can walk, then," she said, wiping at her eyes.

"I know," he teased softly, "but I am attempting to rescue you, so please indulge me."

"Your Grace?"

"Jack, will you be so kind as to carry Miss Ralston up to her bedchamber for me?" he asked, rising again.

"With pleasure, Your Grace."

Jack stepped into the room and lifted Katherine's petite form in his arms. Nicholas followed them up the stairs and into the bedchamber she indicated. At the sight of the chain locked to the bedpost he swore long and loudly. "I should have killed him," he snarled, flinging the chain against the wall. Noticing that Jack was still holding Katherine and that both were watching him somewhat nervously, he motioned at the bed. "Set her down, if you please."

The groom did as he asked and stepped away from the bed. "Thank you, Jack," Katherine murmured.

"Find me some bandages and liniment, and be quick about it," Nicholas instructed. "And see if there's another female in the house." The groom nodded and headed out of the room. Nicholas hesitated, then went to the door and shut it.

"Now, my sweet, you must continue to think of me as your guardian angel, for that is all I shall be for the next few moments."

She looked at him, squinting one eye, then nodded. "Yes, Angel."

He helped her out of her gown, dumping the ugly thing into the corner. Her dirty, ripped shift came next, and he growled at the sight of her bruised thigh and shoulder, though his emotions at the sight of the rest of her were far from angry. She was breathtaking. He swiftly helped her under the covers and pulled them up to her neck.

Jack knocked, then opened the door when Nicholas acknowledged him. The groom carried a tray loaded with several strips of cloth, some liniment, and a bowl of clean water. At Nicholas's gesture he set them on the chair by the bed. "Your Grace, the only other person here 'sides us is the cook, and she's snoring downstairs with an empty bottle of port for company." He scowled. "I wouldn't want the likes of her up here."

"Thank you, Jack," Nicholas said. "I'll take care of it, then. Please go see how Gladstone is doing. I want the two of you to see Ralston on the stage to Bristol." He dug more money out of his pocket and handed it to his groom. "And make certain he doesn't get off until he reaches the coast."

"Yes, Your Grace." He started for the door, then hesitated and turned around. "And milady, Your Grace?" he asked hesitantly.

Nicholas frowned. "I shall be a perfect gentleman, Jack. And having two men in here seeing to her injuries would not do her much good."

This time Jack shut the door himself. Nicholas gingerly removed his jacket, dumped it over the back of the chair, and sat on the edge of the bed. Katherine watched as he rolled up his sleeves.

"This will likely hurt like the devil," he said apologetically, putting a small measure of laudanum in a glass and holding her up to drink it.

He pulled her left hand out from under the covers and, gently as he could, cleaned the rope burns and cuts. He then smeared liniment over the bruises and bound her wrist firmly with the clean cloth. He repeated the process with her right wrist, and then, after a hesitation, pulled the covers down below her shoulders.

"Are you certain you're a guardian angel?" she asked, trying to smile and failing miserably, her eyes on his face.

He cleared his throat. "You have no idea what a challenge this is for me, but yes, I remain faithfully so."

He rubbed more liniment into the bruise on her shoulder, and covered it loosely with a cloth. He pulled the covers up again, then stood and raised the sheets up on her left side to expose her thigh. Again he rubbed liniment into the angry purple bruise and lightly wrapped a cloth around her leg, so the oily stuff wouldn't come off onto the bed sheets.

That done, he covered her again and removed the medicines to her dressing table before he returned to her side to gaze down at her face. The lines of worry had eased, and she was nearly asleep. He supposed he shouldn't have found it terribly flattering that a woman could doze off while he touched her so intimately, but the obvious trust she showed him affected him deeply. Unable to resist, he leaned forward and brushed his lips against her forehead.

"Nicholas?" she said sleepily.

"Yes?" he responded, wearily sinking back down into the chair.

"Did you call me your 'love,' earlier?"

"Yes, I did," he answered after a hesitation. Lord, she unsettled him.

"I thought so," she murmured, smiling, and then was asleep.

Nicholas tended to her ankles, and then sat watching over her for a long time. Here he was, alone at Crestley

Hall with a beautiful woman lying naked only a few feet away, completely at his mercy, and he was behaving like a perfect gentleman. And with no witnesses to be impressed by his self-restraint. He must be in love, he reflected with a smile. Only that could make him act so utterly stupid.

15

"Good morning."

Katherine sat up stiffly and looked toward the window, to see Nicholas sitting in the deep sill. He was still in his shirt sleeves, and, from the look of him, hadn't left her side all night. "Good morning," she answered, feeling abruptly shy and wondering how he had gotten her into a clean shift without waking her up.

"How do you feel?" he asked, leaving his seat and walking over to stuff several pillows behind her so she could lean back.

"Much better," she answered, smiling at him.

"Your uncle is gone," he told her, sitting in the chair beside her, "and Gladstone says he seemed to accept the idea that he wouldn't be returning. He won't be bothering you again."

She agreed. The chance for Simon Ralston to profit there had been removed thanks to Nicholas Varon's name on the deed, and so he would have no reason to remain, or to return. "Thank you again."

"You're welcome, though I know how opposed you were to signing Crestley over. We had no luck in coming up with an alternative solution that wouldn't give your uncle a reason to torment you later." He sat back and chuckled. "My man, Gladstone, has a talent for subversiveness

I never suspected. I'm certain he could be a master criminal if he wished."

"As could you, no doubt," she noted, grinning.

"Do you think so?" he queried, raising an eyebrow. "I did rather enjoy the results of our efforts." He sobered, reaching over to take her hand and caress her bandaged wrist. "The price was too high, however, and I think I shall have to keep to tamer pursuits in the future." He grinned wickedly. "Slightly tamer."

Gladstone scratched at the door, and Nicholas rose to open it. The duke's man of business entered, carrying a tray laden with what smelled like toast and potato soup. "Good morning, Your Grace . . . milady. There isn't much in the kitchen," he explained as he placed the tray on the nightstand, "so I put together what looked edible. Jack has gone into the village to buy some things."

"Gladstone," Nicholas exclaimed as his man turned to leave, "another talent. You have the makings of a fine cook."

"Thank you, Your Grace, but I have already found employment I rather enjoy," he replied, bowing as he left the room.

"You shouldn't tease him so, Nicholas," Katherine admonished, only to have him turn his attention back on her.

"It is one of my major goals in life to see Gladstone crack a smile," the Black Duke responded, returning to the chair and picking up the bowl of soup. "A bit below my station," he muttered, dipping the spoon into the hot liquid, "but I think I can manage this."

"Nonsense," she returned. "I can feed myself."

He shrugged and handed over the soup bowl. "As you wish."

She took a mouthful, watching him watching her. "I don't need you to watch me eat, either," she shot back, setting aside the bowl when he showed no sign of leaving.

Finally he sighed and rose. "Well, at least you appear to be feeling better," he noted, and walked to the door. "I'm right next door. If you need me, throw something at the wall."

"Very amusing," she retorted, tempted to throw something at him instead.

The Black Duke grinned, gave a stiff bow, which abruptly reminded her that he was wounded as well, and left the room. The door clicked shut behind him, leaving her alone.

She had begun to realize that he intentionally provoked her, likely just to see how she would react. And she enjoyed it immensely, enjoyed the challenge of matching wits with him, and enjoyed seeing the amused appreciation in his eyes when she scored a hit. It was at Crestley two months earlier that she had given up her dream of a white knight. And here a few hours ago she had realized that perhaps black knights were more interesting, and that perhaps she had found one. She couldn't say exactly when she had fallen in love with Nicholas Varon, but now that she recognized that she had, it seemed it had always been so.

She finished her soup, and then experimentally rose and walked about the bedchamber. She was stiffer than she had been the day before, but the sharp pain in her wrists and ankles was gone, and she could almost feel the liniment working.

Someone knocked quietly at the door, and Nicholas entered before she could answer. He stopped as he saw her standing there. "Sorry to intrude," he said, "but I thought you might be asleep, and I didn't want to wake you. I should have realized you'd be preparing for a hike in the country."

He had put on a clean shirt and waistcoat, and his cravat was tied in a simple knot. She found herself looking at him closely, as though she had never seen him before. Again she took in his lean, broad-shouldered frame, the black, wavy hair that touched his collar, and those emerald-highlighted gray eyes that had begun twinkling at her again.

"What is it—have I grown a third eye?" he asked, raising an eyebrow.

She blushed and turned toward the window. "I was just thinking you must be exhausted," she lied.

"I could do with some sleep." He stepped past her toward the wardrobe. "Do you feel like coming downstairs for a few moments?"

"All right," she agreed, "but I can choose my own clothes, thank you very much." She picked a blue muslin and pulled it on over her shift. She did let him lace the dress up the back, for, stiff as she was, she never would have been able to do it. Wryly she noted the ease with which he performed the task; he seemed to have a great deal of experience with the fastenings on women's clothing.

"Finished," he said after a moment, and took her shoulders to turn her around. "Have you looked out the window yet?" he asked abruptly, frowning a little as he glanced toward the casement.

"No," she said, shaking her head. "I was going to, when you came in. Why?" Abruptly she realized just how long she had been away. She could only imagine what Crestley must look like now.

"Just remember," he said, taking her hand and leading her to the door, "whatever you see, we can make it right. I did purchase the entire Crestley estate, so you now have a great deal of money at your disposal."

The two of them went downstairs, and Nicholas opened the front door. "Where's Timms?" Katherine asked, abruptly missing the butler.

"Apparently your uncle let the entire staff go, except for the one woman who had been coming down from the village to cook. I think she had been stealing, and I took the liberty of letting her go."

"Can we get them back?" The members of the staff had been at Crestley for years. When her uncle had begun dismissing them it had been like losing more of her family.

"Give Gladstone their names, and we'll see what can be done," Nicholas replied.

Once outside, she realized what he had meant. The drive was ugly and rutted, and the lush ivy that had trailed up the walls was dead and tangled at the base of the stones. They had to walk through part of the garden to get to the stables, and weeds twisted among and lifted the stepping stones. All of the roses were dead. Crestley had been neglected since her mother's illness, but Kate was appalled at how far the estate had deteriorated in only a few short months.

They found the duke's bay coach horses staked out in front of the stables, with Jack inside, trying to repair one of the stalls. "Couldn't leave 'em in here, Your Grace," he said. "There's a nest of rats in the loft, and the hay's gone bad."

"Where're the horses?" Katherine asked, dismayed. "My horses, I mean?"

Nicholas tightened his grip on her hand. "Your uncle sold them off, but Gladstone managed to purchase all of them back. They're at Sommesby, in my stables. And quite a fine lot, from what I hear."

"I suppose I should thank you, then," she said quietly, feeling that events had turned far out of her control, and that she was at the mercy of scheming uncles and roguish dukes.

"If you wish," he answered, seeming to sense her mood, "but it's not necessary."

She cleared her throat. "What about the tenant lands?"

"According to Gladstone they could be worse," Nicholas replied, following her back toward the house. "The acreage is a bit overgrown, but the crop still seems to be all right. Your uncle wasn't destructive, just negligent."

"No need to look after something if you don't intend to keep it, I suppose," she murmured, dismayed to realize that she was crying.

Nicholas turned her around and hugged her. "I told you that you needn't worry," he said into her hair.

For a moment she simply stood and let him hold her, putting her arms about his waist to pull him to her in return. "I gave that money back to you," she replied after a moment, understanding what he was referring to. That was one thing she refused to give ground on. "My feelings remain the same. I want no money changing hands where Crestley Hall is concerned. It wouldn't be right."

He was silent for a moment. "Well, then, consider that Crestley has suffered a blight, and allow me to loan you enough to set everything to rights again."

"Why did you gamble the Viscount of Worton's land away from him?" She finally trusted him where Crestley was concerned, but it was important that she know, especially with her home in his hands now, and especially because she had fallen in love with him.

He looked down. "Because I was drunk, and angry, and because he was draining so much money out of Worton that his tenants were starving."

"But you gave the deed to a footman."

"Yes, I did. It wasn't at all legal, though, and Phillips, the footman, is now overseeing Worton while the viscount makes improvements to it, at which time Phillips will return the deed to him." He sighed. "The conclusion isn't nearly as dramatic a tale as the beginning, I'm afraid, so it hasn't circulated nearly as widely."

"So you are occasionally pleasant," she commented, and he smiled.

"Depends who you ask, I suppose."

"I accept your offer of a loan, but I intend to repay it as soon as Crestley is up and running again." There was still money held in her trust, but that wouldn't be accessible for another two years. She wouldn't make him wait that long.

"That's the spirit," he said approvingly, leaning down to kiss her forehead.

She tilted her face up further, for it wasn't her forehead that she wanted kissed. He grinned and bent his head to comply. Katherine closed her eyes, but when she didn't feel his mouth touch hers, she opened them again. Nicholas was looking down at her, a wry grimace on his face.

"What is it?"

"There's no one about to stop me," he answered softly. "Despite my best efforts I fear that I am becoming sadly proper, after all." He looked as though he wanted to say something further, but at the sound of a coach in the drive they both started. "Neville and Alison, I would assume," he said, and took her hand again.

He was correct. As they came around the corner Lord Neville was helping Lady Alison to the ground. "Kate, you are all right," Lady Alison cried, hurrying forward and drawing her into a tight embrace.

Lord Neville followed, and hugged her tightly as well. "I'm so sorry, child," he said. "I never thought Simon Ralston would kidnap his own niece."

"It's all right," she answered, knowing that he had done what he thought was best for her. "If Nicholas hadn't come to buy Crestley, someone else would have, and my uncle still would have needed to bring me here. And everything has worked out." She glanced up at Nicholas.

At that her godfather turned to Sommesby. "You told me you would find her," he said, reaching out his hand. "What's happened with Ralston?"

Nicholas promptly shook the older man's hand. "He has been persuaded to visit America. Permanently."

Lord Neville nodded. "And the deed?"

"Nicholas owns Crestley now," Katherine answered, unable to keep the mournful tone out of her voice.

"My name is on the deed," the duke amended. "Katherine is mistress of Crestley Hall."

The next day Nicholas brought Mr. Gladstone into the morning room, where Katherine and Lady Alison sat chatting. "Excuse me, ladies," he said, "but Gladstone and I would like a word with Katherine."

"Of course, Nick," Lady Alison answered, rising with a

smile. "I'd best see what Neville is up to," she said, and exited the room.

Katherine gestured at the couch opposite her, and the two men sat. "What is it?" she asked, curious.

"I am placing Gladstone at your disposal," Nicholas said, and the secretary nodded. "As you know, he is quite resourceful. He has had twenty years of experience with Sommesby and the other Varon estates, so tell him what you desire, and he will find a way to do it." With a smile Nicholas rose and headed for the door.

Until that moment she hadn't been aware that he owned more than the huge estate at Sommesby, and again she was struck by how powerful the Black Duke must be. "You aren't going to stay?" she asked, looking after him.

He shook his head. "I don't intend to interfere," he answered. "If you desperately need my opinion, however, I shall be in the stables with Jack, chasing rats."

She spent two hours with Gladstone. It was odd to realize that she could do with Crestley Hall whatever she wished, from improvements to restoration to complete reconstruction of the stables. Gladstone indeed knew his business, and after he seemed to realize she would welcome his opinion, he gave it to her in precise and honest terms.

By morning the repairs had begun. Katherine rose early and went downstairs to be greeted at the door by Timms, standing at the ready as though he had never been gone. "Timms!" she exclaimed, delighted, and he gave her a nod and a smile.

"It's good to see that you've come back to set everything to rights, Miss Kate," he said, pulling open the door for her.

Outside she found Nicholas already up and walking along the drive with several workmen from the village. He looked up and greeted her with a smile. "Good morning, Miss Ralston." He excused himself from the villagers and strolled over to her side.

"Good morning, Your Grace," she answered.

"How do you feel this morning?"

"Much better," she answered. "The stiffness is almost gone."

He nodded. "Jack's gone into town to post your letter to Lyman and Chesterpot, the garden supply company. Roses?"

She nodded. "I want the garden to be back the way it was."

"Your parents would be pleased, I think."

She smiled a little tearfully. "Thank you."

He touched her cheek with his fingers. "Cheer up, Kate. Jack and I have decimated the stable's rat population for you, at great hazard to ourselves, and I'll send to Sommesby for your horses as soon as you wish it."

"My heroes," she said with a chuckle, and he raised an eyebrow.

"Such a cynic, you are."

"It's a habit I've picked up from you," she responded with a grin. She stayed outside for most of the morning while more villagers arrived to begin pulling out the dead growth around the manor and filling in the potholes in the drive.

When she went back inside and sat down to a light lunch with Lady Alison, her godmother finally asked her what had transpired at Crestley before her arrival. "But who bandaged your wrists and treated your other bruises?" her godmother asked at the finish, though from her tone Katherine assumed she knew the answer.

"Nicholas did," she replied.

"Nick treated your wounds?" Lady Alison repeated. For a long moment she looked closely at her goddaughter, and Katherine steadily returned her gaze.

"There was no one else here to do it," she said.

"Yes, and that is what I fear everyone will realize," the baroness responded.

"What?" Katherine asked, feeling a twinge of uneasiness at her godmother's somber tone.

"That you and the Black Duke of Sommesby were, for

all intents and purposes, alone together at Crestley for better than a day."

"But he's been behaving like an old sobersides," Katherine protested. "He has done nothing improper. Nothing. And neither have I."

Lady Alison reached over and gripped her goddaughter's fingers. "I believe you, Kate. But I'm not the one who matters. It is the rest of the *ton* who will judge."

"If they believe that anything has happened, then they are a great gab of muttonheads, and I don't care what they might think." With that, she rose and left the room.

So her godmother thought that she had been ruined. If that was the case, and society would no longer accept her, then she would simply remain at Crestley Hall, though the notion of staying there, alone and without Nicholas to talk to her and to make her laugh, wasn't nearly as appealing as it had been two months earlier. But there still were several days before they all planned to return to London. Perhaps they could figure something out in time. They had been successful with their schemes thus far.

16

The Duke of Sommesby knew that by now Katherine was ruined. Polite society shrank from any scandal, whoever actually happened to be at fault. Even if some paragon of virtue such as the Viscount of Sheresford or Captain Reginald Hillary had come after her, there would have been little chance to repair the damage. With the Black Duke as rescuer, there was no hope at all.

If he had needed a reason to marry her other than the fact that he was desperately in love with her, her unexpected removal to Crestley had provided him with one. He had begun that venture thinking only that he was purchasing a piece of property for a friend. He had had no idea that the prize, the true prize, would be a beautiful black-haired madcap with a quick tongue and a quicker wit. She was worth any price, any inconvenience, including having her shoot him, although he wished to avoid that happening again if possible.

On the morning of their fifth day at Crestley he rose early, as he usually did when he was in the country, and headed downstairs to the breakfast room to find Neville and Alison. "Good morning," he said with a smile.

"Good morning," Neville returned. "Your color is much better. I think the country air agrees with you."

"I think it's just that being shot disagrees with me," he

144

replied with a grin as he took a seat. "Is Katherine awake yet?"

Alison nodded. "Yes. She and Jack have gone down to the village to look into the purchase of lumber to rebuild the stables."

"Do you intend to return to London soon?" Neville asked as he passed a basket of hot biscuits. The cook Gladstone had found was a treasure.

Nicholas nodded. "I think it best if we all did. A united front, as it were."

"Nick," Alison said abruptly, setting down her tea, "we know you have behaved properly toward Kate, and I know she thinks she will be able to handle any rejection from society, but I don't think she realizes what that really means. I think it will hurt her a great deal."

Nicholas nodded, agreeing. He remembered how alone Katherine had seemed when she first arrived in town, something he had sensed when he saw her empty dance card at the Albey ball. He tilted his head at her godparents, both now looking at him hopefully. "I intend to take care of things," he said by way of answer, and then leaned forward. "How do you know I have been behaving properly? I almost never do."

The baroness smiled. "Kate said you'd been acting like an old sobersides."

In his entire life no one had ever accused him of such a thing, and he stared at Alison, stunned into silence. Finally he gave a shout of laughter. "Oh, good God." He chuckled. "I shall have to remedy that immediately." He rose and excused himself from the table.

While he waited for Katherine to return, he went to find Gladstone. He closeted himself with his secretary for several hours, for between Crestley Hall, being shot, and the distraction of Katherine, he had recently fallen somewhat behind with matters regarding his own properties. Gladstone brought him up to date, and then informed him of several of the innovations that Katherine was planning, including a new irrigation system that his secretary had been trying unsuccessfully to talk Nicholas into installing at Sommesby for years.

Afterward he went outside to find that Katherine had returned and was pacing around the outside of the stable, eyeing it critically. As she turned around to greet him, Nicholas stepped forward and wiped a streak of dirt off her nose with his thumb. "I wish I could write poetry," he murmured, "because saying that you are beautiful simply does you no justice."

Her eyes twinkling, she turned away to head back to the manor. "I think you might be more of a poet than you confess."

Grinning, he followed her. "I thought I was an old sobersides. The two hardly seem compatible."

She stopped and turned to face him, flushing. "Lady Alison told you I said that?"

He nodded. "Very unflattering." She continued to look embarrassed, so he glanced away toward the field. "Are you certain you want to try a whole new irrigation system on something the size of Crestley?" he asked. "You'll be using up good planting ground."

She was silent for a moment. "I thought you weren't going to interfere," she finally said.

"Suggesting isn't interfering," he countered, taking a step toward her and wondering how in the world he was going to get around to the subject of asking her to marry him.

She turned away and started back toward the house. "You said that Gladstone was at my disposal."

"So I did." She was getting angry about something, and whatever she was implying, he didn't like it.

"You didn't tell me he would be acting as your spy."

"He's not my spy."

Kate turned around again, hands on her hips. "You said he had a talent for such things."

He frowned. "Yes, I did. But I didn't send him to spy on you, for Lucifer's sake."

"Then how is it that you know everything I'm planning

here? And why do you think you know more about Crestley Hall than I do?"

She had gotten it all wrong, and now he was angry as well. "I don't. And that's not fair, Kate."

"Oh?" she snapped, folding her arms across her chest. "And why not?"

"You'll take my money, but not my opinion?"

She didn't back down. "If that's part of your bargain, then I'll take neither. You said Crestley was still mine. I can manage quite well, without your money and without your assistance. I certainly don't need you to feed me and clothe me, or to tell me which of my—*my*—projects you approve of."

"That's enough, Kate," he said warningly.

"What, will you withhold the deed until I've made improvements that meet your approval?" she retorted. "You're worse than Uncle Simon, trying to ruin what belongs to me and telling me it's for my own good."

"You need some manners, you shrew," he flung back at her.

She went white. Abruptly she flung her hand out, catching him full on the left cheek with her open palm. The blow stung, but far more stupefying was the fact that she had actually struck him.

She looked stunned as well, but stood her ground. "I have only one question for you, Your Grace," she ground out.

"Yes, Miss Ralston?" he returned stiffly.

"Is Crestley Hall still considered to be my property to manage?" she asked, her voice shaking. "Or are you going to hand my deed over to some shepherd?"

"Crestley is yours, Miss Ralston," he affirmed, so angry, his own voice was unsteady.

"Then get off my property."

For a moment he was again too stunned to speak. "As you wish," he was finally able to reply, and turned his back to stride away from her.

He headed for the stables, where Jack was busy hammering at something. "Jack!" he bellowed. "Put that damn thing down and get the coach ready! We are leaving for London."

"Your Grace?" his groom said questioningly, sticking his head out of one of the stalls.

"Now, Jack!"

"Yes, Your Grace."

Back inside the house he found Gladstone and told him he was to remain until he was satisfied that Crestley was being properly restored, and he was then to hire a coach and take himself back to London. His secretary agreed without comment. Upstairs Nicholas threw his things back into the traveling cases he had unpacked less than a week earlier. That done, he brought the cases downstairs himself, not willing to wait for the damned doddering old butler to do it.

Neville and Alison were going through the disorganized mass of papers in the drawing room when he strode in. "I am taking my leave of you," he said, and turned around again.

"Nick, what's going on?" Alison queried, standing up in alarm.

"Ask your darling Kate," he spat out, and walked out, slamming the door behind him. He couldn't believe that he had been on the verge of asking that damned stubborn, impossible, ungrateful woman to marry him. He would sooner wed . . . He couldn't think of anyone who made him as angry as she, and so he grabbed up his cases again, swearing. He didn't stop cursing until he was well on the road back to London.

17

Katherine stayed away from the house for better than an hour. When she finally returned she had calmed down, and half expected to see Nicholas waiting for her, ready to fly up into the boughs at her for slapping him and behaving like such a gudgeon. He was maddeningly overbearing, but belatedly she had realized that he had only been trying to assist her. And perhaps she did need him a little, not for his considerable wealth, but for the way he made her feel.

Instead of Sommesby, though, she found her godparents sitting in the parlor. They looked at her as though some great tragedy had befallen them all. "Oh, dear," Lady Alison said, taking Kate's hand and drawing her down to the couch.

"What is it?" Katherine asked, bewildered and more than a little worried.

"Whatever did you say to Nick?" her godmother asked earnestly.

Katherine lowered her eyes. "I told him to get off my property."

"You said that to the Duke of Sommesby?" Neville queried, raising his brow.

Lady Alison gasped. "How could you do such a thing?"

"He made me angry," Katherine stated, "trying to order

me about and telling me what to do as if I were one of his footmen."

"But what about—"

Katherine sighed and stood. "Where is he? I suppose I have to apologize."

"He's gone back to London," Lord Neville said when his wife put one hand over her face.

"He's gone back . . ." Katherine sat down rather abruptly, feeling as though the breath had been knocked out of her lungs. "Well, good. Good riddance," she said, her voice breaking. Nicholas was gone. She knew he had been angry, but they had argued before. She had never thought he would leave.

"Did you refuse him?" her godmother asked softly.

"Refuse him?" Katherine echoed, beginning to feel hysterical.

"He was going to offer for you," Neville explained.

Kate's heart faltered. "Nicholas was going to ask me to marry him?" she whispered.

"Yes, child." Lady Alison tried to take her hand again, but she pulled away.

"Well, I wouldn't have married him, anyway. I could never marry such an arrogant, provoking man."

"I'm so sorry, Kate," her godmother murmured.

"Don't be," she said, shooting to her feet and hurrying toward the door, so they wouldn't see her crying. "I'm glad he's gone. I hope I never see him again."

He had gone back to London. The Black Duke had changed his mind about her and left. He'd probably never even give her another thought. He'd probably already found someone else to tease and send roses to, if he even bothered with such things where his other conquests were concerned. Katherine looked for any excuse to remain at Crestley, but after a week her godparents finally told her in no uncertain terms that they were returning to London. They were concerned about her reputation, but she dreaded seeing Nicholas again more than she felt trepidation about encountering the snubs of the *ton*.

They arrived back in town with no ceremony, and Katherine spent the next days moping about Hampton House and trying to pretend that she was not. From the reaction of her godparents she knew something wasn't right, and she realized that no one had come to call, or even sent a card. "I told you it doesn't matter," she said to Lady Alison when her godmother appeared close to tears after their third day back. "Just let me return to Crestley."

"No, my dear. If anything is to be done to salvage this situation, we must act now. We shouldn't have stayed away even this long." She shook her head. "Oh, if only Nick hadn't ridden back here like that. He must have known this would happen."

"I'm certain he didn't care."

"You don't mean that, Kate."

"Yes, I do." She had known better, had been warned innumerable times about the notorious Black Duke, and she had been a ninnyhammer and fallen for him anyway. And now she was paying the price.

Despite Kate's protests, the baroness decided that they should go shopping. It would get them both outside, her godmother argued, and perhaps they would find that things were not as bad as they had imagined.

Things were as bad as they had imagined. Once-unctuous dressmakers were barely civil, a sure sign that her story had been widely bandied about. Katherine was certain that if she hadn't been with Lady Alison she never would have been waited on at all. Several ladies in the shops left as they entered, the younger ones staring at her with bald curiosity as they went.

Lady Alison continued to claim that it didn't signify, but her protestations became more and more muted, and finally she suggested that they return to Hampton House, after all. Outside a dressmaker's her godmother stopped short. A beautiful brunette woman walked toward them along the street, her eyes so dark, they looked black. Her dark blue dress was of the finest muslin, and her skin like porcelain. She stopped before Kate with a rustle of skirts.

"You are Kate Ralston," the woman stated with a heavy French accent.

Lady Alison took Kate's arm and tried to turn her away, but Katherine was intrigued. "I am," she replied.

"You are barely more than a child," the woman murmured. "Not at all the one for Nick. I am surprised he did not realize so much sooner."

"Go away," Lady Alison snapped, pushing Katherine toward the carriage.

The woman nodded. "I hope he at least gave you a nice parting gift. He does that, for the ones who amuse him."

Lady Alison instructed their driver to leave immediately. "Don't look after her, Kate," she ordered.

"Who is she?" Katherine asked, looking over at her godmother's white face. She had never seen Lady Alison so angry.

"Josette Bettreaux. I thought her still in Paris. She *would* come back now."

"That was Josette Bettreaux?" Katherine echoed feebly. Louisa had been right. The woman was stunning.

When they returned to Hampton House Katherine was little heartened to see the Viscount of Sheresford's phaeton there before them. When Rawlins opened the door he informed her that the viscount had arrived several minutes earlier and was waiting for her in the drawing room. Her godmother sighed, then motioned for Kate to go meet him.

When she entered, Thomas was pacing up and down as though he were being chased. "Thomas, is something wrong?" she asked.

"Kate, I'm so pleased you're home safe," he said, coming to her and taking her hands.

Privately she thought that if he had been that concerned he could have come to see her two days before, but she said nothing. She was in dire need of a friend, and he was the only one who had shown himself. "Quite safe," she replied.

He released her and strode away, then turned around again. "I would have come sooner, but I had . . . there was business I had to tend to."

"I understand." She seated herself.

"Kate," he went on, walking over to the mantel and leaning on it, then striding over to the window, "I need to know something before I go on. I hope you understand."

She nodded, wishing that he would stop moving around so much, for he was making her dizzy.

"Did anything transpire between you and Nick while you were away?"

She started to retort that it was none of his business, but he seemed so genuinely concerned that she relented. "We argued," she replied with a shrug.

"That was all?" he pursued, coming closer.

"That was enough," she answered. Enough to ruin her, and enough to break her heart.

He nodded. "Nick's been in a rare temper since he came back to town. Right after he returned I asked him how you were, but he only glared at me until I thought he was going to kill me."

"I really don't care to hear about him," Katherine said stiffly. "May I ask you a question now?"

"Of course." He took a seat, but she doubted that he would light for long.

"When did Josette Bettreaux return to town?"

The viscount shot to his feet. "How do you know that name?"

"She spoke to me this morning when Lady Alison and I were out shopping."

"She didn't!" He gasped, his expression mortified.

"She did. And not very kindly."

Thomas cleared his throat, and for a moment she thought that he wouldn't answer. "She came back two days after you . . . left for Crestley," he finally said.

Katherine felt like crying, and took a deep breath to steady herself. "Is he seeing her again?"

"It depends on who you ask," Thomas said shortly.

"According to Josette he is; according to Nick it's no one's bloody business." He came forward again and sat beside her, taking her hand in his. "I didn't come here to discuss Nick either, however."

"No?" Katherine asked, wondering whether Nicholas looked at the lovely Josette and his other mistresses in the same way that he had looked at her, and whether his parting gift to her for amusing him had been the return of Crestley Hall.

"No. I've come to ask you to be my wife." Abruptly Thomas was on his knees in front of her, his eyes on her face and his expression earnest.

"To marry you?" Katherine repeated, completely astonished.

"I know that you don't love me," he went on hurriedly, "but I'm certain that you could grow to." She opened her mouth, but he kept going. "Don't answer now. Think about it, please. All right?"

"Are you doing this to try to save my reputation?" she asked, smiling sadly.

He cleared his throat again. "Not entirely."

"And are you aware that Althaea Hillary has been in love with you for quite some time?"

He stood again, blushing wildly. "Althaea? She's not—" Katherine nodded. "She is."

Obviously flustered, Thomas began pacing about the room again. "I don't mean to back out," he said abruptly. "Say that you will seriously consider my offer."

"I will seriously consider your offer," she affirmed.

"Well, then, I shall take my leave of you." He started for the door, then hesitated, turned back, and leaned down to kiss her lightly on the lips. "Good day, Kate."

"Good day, Thomas."

She sat in the drawing room for a long time after the viscount left. If she had had any doubts before about her feelings for Thomas, the kiss had answered them for her. He was a friend, and she would never be able to think of him as anything else. And, unless she missed her guess, her friend was in love with Althaea Hillary.

Finally Lady Alison knocked and entered the room. "What did Thomas want?"

"He asked me to marry him," Katherine replied, glancing up at the baroness.

"He asked—oh, Kate, that's wonderful!" Her godmother came forward and took her hand, but her smile faded when it became apparent that Katherine didn't share her enthusiasm. "You turned him down, didn't you?" she said after a moment.

"Not yet," Katherine replied, "but I mean to."

"But why?"

"Because I don't love him, and because he's in love with someone else. I won't buy my respect with someone else's happiness."

Alison sighed. "Well, I suppose it's not as bad as it could be," she said with a slight smile. The baroness displayed a letter. "We've been invited to Julia Varon's for tea tomorrow afternoon. If anyone can help this situation, she can."

The invitation to go to tea at his mother's had immediately aroused Nicholas's suspicions, and he had sent a polite but firm refusal. She likely wanted to discuss his flight from Crestley Hall, and he had no desire to do so. Especially not with her.

He had already asked Josette Bettreaux to go riding with him, anyway. When she had arrived at Varon House the night after his return from Crestley, he had been surprised. It had seemed a lifetime longer than three months since their rather violent parting, and as she entered the library and kissed him he realized that he hadn't given her a thought since he had met Katherine Ralston. Still not quite ready to forgive her, he had rather brusquely sent her away. But neither was he quite ready to forgive Kate, and so over the ensuing days he had taken Josette to the opera and even on a picnic.

As he looked over at her now, exquisite in a black riding habit the color of her eyes, he wondered if she wasn't there to punish him rather than Kate. She had apologized, several times, for the incident at the Josten ball, but he didn't trust her. He had never trusted her, but in the past her company had been pleasant, and she had been unobtrusive as far as his time and his mind were concerned.

Now, though, he was finding her acquiescence somewhat annoying. She wanted nothing except what he wanted, or so she said. She had only pestered him about one thing, and it was the one thing he denied her. Despite all of her skills at seduction, he had stayed out of her bedchamber. He knew she didn't understand why, but he knew all too well. Despite his best efforts he couldn't forget Katherine Ralston.

He looked up at the sound of someone calling his name. Thomas Elder rode toward him on Orpheus, and beneath him Ulysses snorted in recognition of his chief rival. Nicholas felt somewhat like doing the same. "Thomas." He nodded.

"May I speak to you for a moment?" The young viscount glanced pointedly over at Josette, who sat looking at him from beneath her long eyelashes.

"Wait here," Nicholas said to her, then kneed Ulysses away without waiting for a response. "What is it?" he asked when they were out of earshot.

"Were you aware that Kate Ralston has returned to London?"

Nicholas became very still and looked down at Ulysses' left ear. "No, I was not," he said after a moment, trying to ignore what the mere mention of the dratted chit's name was doing to his heart rate.

"Then you aren't aware that she is being snubbed by everyone, and that your lovely Josette accosted her on the street yesterday and, from what I have been able to determine, was exceedingly rude to her?"

The young man was obviously furious. Feeling more

than a spark of anger, Nicholas glanced over at Josette.
"No, I was not aware of it," he replied.

"I wanted you to know that I've asked Kate to be my
wife," Sheresford continued.

Nicholas's heart dropped out of his chest, and he shut
his eyes for a moment. He forced himself to take a slow
breath. "Has she accepted?" he asked quietly.

"Not yet." Thomas fidgeted with his reins, then looked
over at him. "I hope her delay isn't because of you, for
you don't deserve her after what you've done to her."

"That's enough, Thomas," Nicholas murmured. He
knew damn well what he'd done to Katherine, and he
didn't need this man telling him.

"I'm not so certain it is," the viscount returned stiffly.
"If she accepts me, and if this trouble isn't resolved, I will
call you out over it."

Nicholas looked over at him. Thomas was in earnest,
and at that moment the duke was in the mood to do him
some serious injury. "I'll be waiting."

Thomas slapped the end of his reins against his thigh.
"Dammit, Nick, take care of it. I don't want you blowing
my head off because the two of you can't manage to fall
in love peacefully."

Nicholas glared at him until the viscount began to fid-
get. Damn him, the man was right. "You're a better friend
than I deserve, Thomas," he said finally.

"Just remember that if I end up facing you in some field
over this." The viscount gave a short grin and nodded
stiffly at Josette as he departed.

Nicholas returned to her side and reined in Ulysses.
"What did you say to Kate Ralston yesterday?" he murmured.

"Only that she was not right for you, *mon cher,*" Josette
responded.

"You had no right, Josette," he spat out, furious.

"And why not?" she returned, lifting her head to look
directly at him. "I give you what you want, and you give
me what I want. I must protect that, yes?"

He stared at her for a long moment. "Is that why you sent that boy to shoot me?"

She smiled. "You were taking me for granted. It gave me your attention, no? And now we are together again."

That was likely the most honest thing she had ever said to him. Perhaps he and Josette deserved each other. Especially after what he had done to Kate. "We go to the Duffshire ball tonight," he said. "I'll come by for you at eight."

She gave a faint smile. "I will be ready." It was her turn to look closely at him, until finally she nodded. "Is this because you wish to go with me, or because you wish her to see that you are not alone?"

Surprised again, Nicholas looked off across the park. "I don't know, Josette."

"No? We will find out tonight, I think."

He sighed and turned Ulysses around. "Yes, we likely will."

18

"**M**y son is usually very wise," the Dowager Duchess said as Kate finished relating the events of the past two weeks, "but in this instance I think he has been a great fool." She leaned forward and poured herself another cup of tea, looking over at Kate, beside her.

"Thank you, Your Grace," Katherine said, uncertain about whether she was supposed to respond.

Julia nodded. "Unfortunately, I have never been able to tell him what to do. He is too like his father, and must always find things out for himself." She picked up an envelope and handed it to Lady Alison. "Nicholas I can do nothing about. But I can try to fix what he has done to you."

Alison opened the envelope. She pulled out an engraved parchment and then smiled. "Thank you, Julia."

She showed it to Kate. It was an invitation to the Duffshire ball that evening. "Thank you, Your Grace," Kate echoed, giving a small smile.

"It will be a terrible night, but you will manage." She patted Kate on the knee. "You will because you must."

Nicholas entered the ballroom with Josette on his arm and ignored the looks and murmurs of the guests nearest them. He didn't know if Katherine would be in attendance, but he would let her know who needed whom. Josette had dressed in red and black, and looked exquisite even for her. The room was large and crowded, and he refused to look about and see whether Kate was there. Instead he led Josette out onto the floor as the first waltz of the evening began.

Halfway through the dance he saw her. She sat on the far side of the room, with no one in attendance but Neville and Alison. She was in the stunning gold silk gown she had worn when she had stopped him in his tracks at the opera, and she wore a wan smile that looked as though it had been pasted on.

The waltz ended, and he escorted Josette back to the edge of the floor as a country dance began. Again no one claimed Kate's hand. He apparently had done a fine job of ruining her. He had been a fool, trying to organize her life at Crestley, when she was so sensitive about the ownership of the estate. He expected everyone to do as he wished because they all needed him for something. Katherine had her own property, and most definitely her own mind, and she needed him for nothing. Perhaps that was what he found so attractive about her. If only he had realized in time that her spirit and her independence were what made her so unique and so precious, and he was wrong to find fault in her for them.

"I wish a diamond bracelet," Josette murmured.

"What?" He turned to look at her.

"My gift, Nicky," she explained. "A diamond bracelet." She pulled her hand free from his arm and glanced over in Katherine's direction. "Time for me to go find another friend, I think." With a slight smile she backed away a step. "And this time I will not send someone to try to shoot you, *mon cher.*"

"Why not, Josette?" he asked.

"These last few days you have spoken to me, and listened to me. This you have never done before. But it is not I who have changed, Nicholas." She turned around and stepped into the crowd. "Good luck," she murmured over her shoulder.

He looked after her for a moment. "Thank you," he returned, though he doubted she heard. She was wrong. He was not the only one who had changed.

With a deep breath, for he knew that whatever was about to transpire would likely give the town wags fodder for years, he made his way across the room. The dance continued, but the attention of most of the guests immediately shifted to him, and soon it seemed as though the dance floor had rather emptied.

"Miss Ralston," he drawled as he came to a stop in front of her.

Kate lifted her head. She knew he had come that night, for she had seen him enter the ballroom with Josette Bettreaux on his arm, but she never expected that he would dare to speak to her. "Go away," she whispered, her voice cracking. "Everyone is staring."

"I'm not going anywhere," he answered. "May I see your dance card?"

She almost didn't give it to him, but he didn't look as though he would leave if she simply ignored him. As he took the paper his fingers brushed hers, and she flinched again. There wasn't much for him to see, for Lord Neville, Thomas, and Reg were the only names on the card.

After a moment Nicholas cleared his throat. "Woefully thin," he managed to say.

"Now, whose fault might that be?" Lord Neville asked sharply.

"Give me your pencil," he demanded, ignoring the baron and holding his hand out again. "I had the devil of a time finding one before."

She handed it to him. "I don't think you'll have as much luck filling it tonight," she muttered, looking away and wishing she had never come. Almost no one had looked at her, much less spoken to her, since she had arrived. And now no one ever would again.

"You have no faith," he answered, taking a seat on the far side of Lady Alison. He wrote for a moment, then rose again and handed it back to her.

She looked down at it, and her mouth quirked. "You can't do that," she retorted, motioning at the card.

"I can do anything I wish," he drawled. "I'm a duke."

"But you've taken up every space," she protested, finally meeting his eyes. "Even for the dances that have already passed."

"What more harm could it do?" he responded. "You're ruined, and I'm a rake, so we may as well enjoy ourselves."

Music for another waltz started up, and he leaned over to look at her card. "I believe this is my dance," he stated, indicating the correct line, and then reached his hand down to her.

After another hesitation she slipped her hand into his, and with a tight nod at her godparents Nicholas led her out onto the deserted dance floor. They danced in silence for a few moments, taking advantage of the space around them. Kate wished he would speak, or do something, before she burst into tears at his closeness.

"I thought you came here with Josette Bettreaux," she finally said, unable to bear the silence any longer.

He nodded. "I did."

"Then how can you claim every dance with me?" she queried.

"Josette and I have . . . parted ways," he said quietly.

"Oh," she commented, hurt and angry that he would even acknowledge being with that woman. She raised her head to look at him straight on. "Did you give her a parting gift?"

She waited for him to lie or to make a sarcastic comment, but for a long time he just looked at her with serious gray eyes. "She asked for a bracelet," he finally said. "I'll send her one in the morning."

"Why didn't I get a gift, then?" Kate challenged, her

lips tight to keep them from trembling. "It seems that after what you've done to me I should get something."

He tightened his grip on her hand, and she thought that she had finally succeeded in making the Black Duke angry again. "I'm not through with you," he murmured, his eyes glinting.

"Oh, so you're not through with me?" she repeated, her voice rising. "This is all your decision, is it? I told you before, I don't need you for—"

"Yes, you do need me," he interrupted with a growl. "Tonight, unless you wish to stay ruined, you need me. Can you admit that, Kate?"

Tears filled her eyes. "I don't want to need you," she whispered. "I don't want to rely on you."

"But you can, Katherine," he whispered back. "Believe me. You can. Let me make this up to you. Please. Because even though you may not need me, I need you."

She had never expected to hear such an admission from him. "You need me?" she repeated.

"Everything is so dull without you, you know," he said softly, then smiled a little. "No one to put me in my place, or to knock me in the head when I say dreadful things."

She smiled back despite herself. "I didn't think you would miss that."

"But I do." He grinned back at her, then sobered again. "Thomas told me he has proposed to you."

"Yes, he has," she confirmed, her spirits lifting a little. He almost sounded jealous. "Quite admirable of him, considering he's in love with Althaea Hillary."

"Thomas in love with Althaea?" he repeated, obviously startled. "That timid little flower?"

Katherine chuckled. "She's only timid around you."

"Me?"

"She's been deathly afraid that you'll offer for her. She thinks you're entirely too fierce."

Nicholas snorted. "I have been called much worse, and mainly by you," he pointed out.

Abruptly she remembered that she was ruined. "What do we do now?" she muttered.

The music had ended, and she turned to leave the floor. He held onto her arm and made her stay. "We dance. The next one is mine as well," he reminded her.

"Don't make me do this," she protested, deeply embarrassed.

Immediately he placed her hand on his arm and led her off the floor. "All right," he acquiesced, "but you must promise that I may call on you tomorrow."

She nodded, and a single tear rolled down her cheek. He reached up and gently brushed it away with his thumb, and she almost leaned up and kissed him, right in the middle of the ballroom. "Tomorrow," she echoed.

"You may rely on me for this," he murmured.

"I will," she answered.

19

Katherine slept through the night for the first time since Nicholas had left Crestley Hall, and she didn't awaken until Emmie pulled open the curtains a little before noon. Her maid seemed to be making as much noise as possible, and finally Katherine gave up feigning sleep and sat up. "What in the world are you doing?"

"Oh, Miss Kate, you must come downstairs," Emmie gushed, coming forward to tug on her arm.

"I'm not dressed," Katherine protested with a sleepy grin as she allowed herself to be pulled from the bed.

"But you must come. I'll get your robe."

Emmie dashed away and returned a few seconds later with her robe, which Katherine shrugged on, trying not to giggle. Whatever was going on, Emmie was certainly very excited about it, and her delight was infectious.

At the landing of the stairs Katherine stopped, gasping. There were roses everywhere. Red roses, white roses, pink and yellow roses stood in a profusion of vases on every available space in the hallway. Her godparents stood at the foot of the stairs, smiling up at her.

"He must have bought out every flower shop in London," Alison murmured.

The scent of roses filled the air as Kate descended the steps, and she took a deep breath and closed her eyes for a moment before she opened them again in wonder. She had never seen so many roses in one place, and when she caught a glimpse of still more vases in the morning room she began to chuckle. "Oh, goodness," she breathed.

"Is there a card?" Lady Alison asked.

They began a laughing search through the profusion of blooms until Katherine found the envelope tucked into a vase full of red buds. Her hands shaking a little, she pulled out the card. In Nicholas's familiar, strong hand it read, "Dearest Katherine, Every petal here a kiss, every thorn a sigh, and every vase a weapon. Love, Nicholas."

She burst into laughter. It was overall a highly improper note to send to a young lady, but it was very like him. She stood staring at the signature for a long time, fascinated by the words *Love, Nicholas.* Abruptly she remembered that he might call on her at any moment, and she hurried upstairs.

She decided to wear the peach muslin that she had worn on their picnic. Emmie fussed over her hair for so long, Kate thought she would go mad from sitting, but then when that was finished she didn't know what to do with herself.

She wandered down to the morning room to find Lady Alison stitching amid the profusion of blooms. After she had fidgeted with all of the vases, turning them this way and that for nearly an hour, her godmother firmly suggested she go out to the garden. She complied, but soon found herself back inside, wandering the hallways, torn between fury at Nicholas for keeping her waiting and worry over what was keeping him. When she heard the front door open she rushed into the entryway, and nearly collided with Louisa.

"Kate?" the young lady exclaimed, startled, then grabbed onto her arms and hugged her, laughing. "I hear that congratulations are due."

Althaea stepped around Rawlins. "How wonderful for you, Kate," she seconded, and kissed Katherine on the cheek.

"I admit," Louisa said, chuckling, "I wasn't certain whether we'd be attending a duel or a wedding."

Katherine frowned and led the way into the drawing room, where she plunked herself down on the couch. "Don't congratulate me yet," she said mournfully, certain now that something was wrong.

Louisa sat beside her. "What in the world do you mean? Everyone's talking about how last night, when the Black Duke danced with you, half the women at the ball began weeping because they realized Nicholas Varon had finally fallen in love and was off the market."

"And about how His Grace purchased every rose in London this morning," Althaea added. "He even persuaded the Countess of Grenville to part with half of the prize blooms in her garden." She glanced about the hallway. "It's fairly evident that this is where the flowers ended up."

"The flowers may have arrived here," Kate said, glancing up again at all the beautiful blooms, "but Nicholas hasn't."

"What?"

"I expected him hours ago," she said with a sniff.

Louisa took her hand. "Something has simply delayed him, then. I'm certain he hasn't changed his mind."

Until that moment Katherine had been certain as well. "I don't know whether I want to kill him or be anxious for him," she grumbled, trying to smile and failing. He had said she could rely on him for this.

"Be anxious for him," a male voice said from the doorway, and she started.

"Thomas?" she said, her heart missing a beat at the sober expression on the viscount's face. "Why?"

"Nick's gone missing."

Nicholas came to, looking up at a ceiling, and, more specifically, rafters. They were covered with dust and cobwebs, and as he tried to remember where in the world he was, a rat scurried across one of the beams, pausing momentarily to look down at him before it continued on its way.

With an effort he lifted his head to its normal upright position on his shoulders. He was in some sort of warehouse; the floor was cluttered with mildewed straw and the remains of crates and broken barrels. He obviously hadn't placed himself there, for his hands and feet were tied to a rather sturdy chair. Judging from the painful throbbing of his skull, whoever had kidnapped him had clubbed him, and had done a bloody fine job of that indeed. He was very late for something, though he couldn't at that moment remember what. Katherine's face flashed in front of his eyes, and he swore. Damn, he was going to be in a lot of trouble.

"Still among the living, Sommesby?" a smooth voice said from behind him.

Nicholas stiffened, realizing that he was already in more than a little trouble. "DuPres."

"Sorry to say I hit you harder than I intended. Couldn't help myself, really. For a moment, though, I wasn't sure whether you'd be able to assist me."

"Assist you?" Nicholas asked, cursing himself for being addlepated and lovestruck enough to let someone as dangerous as Francis DuPres sneak up behind him. He never should have gone after the Countess of Grenville's flowers. "The only assistance you'll receive from me is pointing you in the direction of hell."

"I'm certain you know that route quite well." Francis DuPres moved around in front of him. "And you may lead the way, after I get what I want."

"Which is?"

"Revenge."

"Oh," Nicholas said, not surprised. "Do your best, then."

"I shall." DuPres pulled a piece of parchment from his jacket pocket. "To begin, sign Crestley Hall over to me."

Nicholas could only stare at him. "Forgive my obtuseness," he said after a moment, "but what in the world ever made you think that clubbing me and tying me up was a good way to persuade me to part with Crestley Hall?"

"If you don't—"

"I mean, I hate to be vulgar," Nicholas drawled, interrupting, "but go to the devil." The entire incident had not been amusing to begin with, and now that his head was beginning to clear he was growing more than a little angry. Crestley Hall would stay safe with him until he and Katherine were wed, though that prospect was again looking dim. He would then deed it solely to her and the heirs of her choosing. And nothing short of death would keep him from doing that small thing for her. He twisted his hands again, and the rope started to come loose. One more good pull and he'd be able to wrap his fingers around DuPres's throat.

"We can do worse than club you, Your Grace," came another voice from behind him. What was obviously the muzzle of a pistol was pressed against the back of Nicholas's skull. After a moment his hands were wrenched painfully, and the ropes tightened again.

DuPres looked at him. "As I said, what I truly want is revenge. Crestley Hall would have been an easy way for me to gain more influence with your snobbish friends, but it's hardly a necessity." He leaned forward, his countenance going ugly. "You took my pride, you took Crestley Hall, and you've taken Kate," DuPres said with a snarl. "You ruined me." He smiled, the expression ghastly. "I only wish to do the same to you. To both of you."

"Leave Katherine out of this," Nicholas replied hotly, twisting his hands in the ropes, abruptly more than merely angry.

"You shouldn't trouble yourself about her." DuPres sighed and set the papers down. "I don't even think she likes you. She did try to shoot you. You thought it was Kate, didn't you? I saw that little play. Her shot nearly killed my horse, outside, past the hedge. I'm the one who almost killed you." He hit Nicholas across the face with his fist. "I *should* have killed you."

"You bastard," Nicholas countered, tasting blood from his cut cheek. That was why the shot had twisted him forward. It had come from behind, through the window. His mother had been *right* when she'd invented an assassin. "You're mad."

Old, comfortable black temper seeped back into his bones. In fact, he couldn't remember ever being quite so angry before. When her uncle had taken Kate, he'd had things to do, to prepare for, and the threat had seemed something he could prevent by his actions. This, though, was different. DuPres wanted her, and he had to sit and listen to this madman's twisted schemes, and he didn't like it. Not at all.

DuPres shrugged, his neck vanishing beneath the high points of his shirt. "Perhaps I am mad. Doesn't signify, though." He pulled out a second piece of paper. "This will be delivered to Hampton House in the morning." He took a breath. " 'Dear Miss Ralston, I have returned just this morning from Crestley, and am troubled to inform you that I must meet with you at once regarding an unforeseen complication. If you are unable to come to my offices at 36 Drapney Lane this morning, I will make an attempt to see you at Hampton House this afternoon. Signed, J. B. Gladstone.' "

Of course Katherine wouldn't wait all day for Gladstone to make an appearance at Hampton House. Even if there was some concern over his own disappearance, Nicholas thought, a problem with Crestley would be more than she could ignore. Kate would walk straight into DuPres's trap. "I hope you realize, DuPres, that you hold your death warrant in your hands," Nicholas said coldly.

"You began this, at White's. This is your doing, Sommesby. All of it. But in the end, I will win. And your precious Kate will wish she'd never set eyes on you."

"You underestimate her," Nicholas answered.

Francis shook his head. "A female? I doubt it." He nodded at the man standing over Nicholas's shoulder. "I'll see you in the morning, Sommesby. Reid?"

Before Nicholas could muster a suitably insulting retort, the pistol came down on the back of his skull and he blacked out.

20

By morning Katherine was nearer hysteria than she had ever been in her life. The Baron of Rensport had discovered Ulysses in the hands of a young street urchin just before dusk, but the boy claimed he had found the stallion wandering several miles from Hampton House. Something was wrong, terribly wrong, and if Nicholas was hurt . . . She couldn't even stand to think of it.

Everyone seemed to know that the Duke of Sommesby was missing, and most of the members of the *ton* had appeared on the Hamptons' doorstep during the past twelve hours, ostensibly with a word of comfort, but more likely to make certain they had the latest *on dit* about Nicholas. What a coup to be there if and when word arrived of the Black Duke's demise. Lady Belle of Dorchester had nearly torn her skirts in her hurry to leave after Prince George had sent a note that everything possible was being done to find "Cousin Nicky."

Louisa had stayed with Katherine all night, and without her friend Kate thought she would have gone mad. Her godparents had spent most of the evening and morning trying to fend off her callers, and except for a moment here and there she had seen almost nothing of them. Louisa made her sit down to breakfast, but she could only pick at a piece of dry toast and sip her tea.

"I'm sorry, Louisa, I'm being such a peagoose," she muttered, wiping her eyes.

"Nonsense," Louisa said firmly, putting an arm around her shoulders. "And everything will be all right. I'm certain of it."

"Yes," Thomas said from the doorway. Althaea and Reg entered behind him as he took Kate's fingers. "For all we know, this could be another of Nick's famous stunts, and he'll come riding up to the door at any moment in the company of a caravan of gypsy dancers."

"If that's all this is, then I shall shoot him again," Kate declared, then blanched when Reg raised an eyebrow at her. She had forgotten they didn't know the truth of that episode.

"I thought so," the captain murmured, leaning down to take her hand.

"Please don't tell," she whispered, looking up at him.

He smiled. "No worries, Kate. That's likely what brought the sap-skull to his senses."

"What are you two whispering about?" Louisa queried, raising her own hand and then hitting Reg on the arm when he delayed a moment before taking it.

The captain kissed her knuckles. "I was merely informing Kate that I will be escorting you home and that Thomas and Thaea will stay with her this morning, my sweet."

"That's not necessary," Katherine protested weakly, relieved that they wouldn't be abandoning her.

Louisa kissed her cheek. "Of course it's necessary. We'll be back this afternoon." She turned to Thomas. "Let us know the moment you hear anything."

He nodded. "We will."

For the next two hours Katherine jumped every time Rawlins opened the front door. Julia Varon sent over a note saying that she was staying at Varon House and would immediately inform her if she received any news. Katherine had barely finished relaying the duchess's missive to her companions when Rawlins scratched at the door again. "Good God," Thomas muttered, rising, "doesn't *anyone* have anything better to do than pester you?" When he opened the door, Rawlins wordlessly handed over another note on his silver tray and bowed as he left.

"I think I'll go lie down for a bit," Katherine said with a scowl, as the distinctive voice of Margaret Dooley, the Baroness of Fens, sounded at the front door.

Althaea nodded. "We'll make your excuses," she said with a smile.

"Thank you." Katherine rose and headed out the side door before any of the next round of guests could see her. She paused on the landing of the back staircase to open the note Rawlins had handed her. "Oh, not now," she muttered, feeling what was left of her world caving in around her. If someone as efficient as Gladstone had run into a complication at Crestley, it must be serious indeed. Abruptly she stopped, frowning. Someone as efficient as Gladstone would not have wasted time by sending a note. And he undoubtedly would have known about the Duke of Sommesby's disappearance and would have considered that to be his first priority.

Katherine started back into the drawing room to fetch Thomas, then stopped again at the Baroness of Fens's laugh. There was no time for explanations or excuses. Hurriedly she scribbled a note to her godparents and left "Gladstone's" note sitting next to it on the hall table. Next she hurried into Lord Neville's study and procured his pair of pistols, though she shuddered at the sight of them. The note felt like a trick of some kind, and she was not going to be taken by surprise again. It was someone else's turn for that. She dumped the pistols in her pockets and climbed out the study window into the garden.

The groom looked dismayed when she insisted that he saddle Winter and that she was not waiting for an escort, but Katherine had the feeling that she would find Nicholas at the address she had copied from the letter, and she was not going to wait. They could follow her later. She had a rescue to perform.

He had been waiting for the sound all morning, and when the rusty door squeaked and rattled open Nicholas knew it would be Kate coming in. After regaining consciousness sometime past midnight he had tried to free himself, but that Reid fellow apparently had had a great deal of practice at tying knots, and all Nicholas had succeeded in doing was rubbing his wrists raw. DuPres had arrived after dawn but had only acknowledged his prisoner long enough to make certain the rag tied over his mouth was secure and still jammed halfway down his throat.

Unused to feeling helpless, and terrified for Katherine's safety at the hands of Francis DuPres, Nicholas could only watch as she stepped into the dim warehouse. She walked forward slowly, her tired expression tempered by more than a touch of wariness. It looked as though she had come alone, and he cursed her godparents for not keeping an eye on her. Desperate to warn her, he yelled at the top of his lungs, managing to produce a muffled bellow through the dirty gag, and she turned in his direction with a start.

"Nicholas!" she screamed, and ran toward him.

He felt rather than heard DuPres come up behind him. "Welcome, Kate," the small man said, and lifted a pistol to point it at Nicholas's head. "Stop there, why don't you?" he suggested, as Reid stepped out of the shadows on the left.

Katherine stopped. "Are you all right, Nicholas?" she asked, her voice shaking.

He nodded, and DuPres pulled the gag loose. "Get out now, Kate," Nicholas ordered hoarsely as soon as he could speak.

"I don't think so," DuPres interrupted. "I'm not through with either of you yet." He took a step forward to stand beside Nicholas. "Kate, I'm going to kill the Duke of Sommesby," he said calmly.

"No!" she wailed, taking another step closer.

"Kate, don't—" Nicholas began, but DuPres cuffed him on the side of the head with the barrel of the pistol, and he reeled in the chair.

"I'm not without compassion, however," DuPres continued. "I'll make you a trade."

"Anything," Katherine returned, balling her hands into fists. Fleetingly Nicholas wished she had brought a vase with her.

"Have Sommesby sign the Crestley Hall deed over to me."

"Never," Nicholas said with a growl.

"Crestley . . ." Kate echoed faintly, her face white.

DuPres flashed his repulsive smile. "The Duke of Sommesby or Crestley Hall. You may have one or the other." The pistol pressed against Nicholas's temple. "But not both."

"Nicholas," she whispered.

"Don't do it, Kate. He'll kill me anyway," Nicholas answered, wishing he could hold her, get her away from that place and that madman with his silent henchman before she was hurt.

"You have my word," DuPres said reasonably. "Crestley for Varon. Just tell him to sign it over."

She looked at Nicholas, and with all his might he willed her to turn and run. Instead she turned to DuPres and nodded. "All right."

DuPres motioned to Reid, who strolled over behind Nicholas and freed his right hand. Nicholas clenched it, trying to get enough feeling back into his fingers that he could hit Francis DuPres. The parchment turning the deed over was put in front of him, and he shook his head. "No."

"Nicholas, sign it," Katherine urged unsteadily.

"No. It's all you've ever wanted. I won't sign it away," he returned, taking a swipe at DuPres. Reid grabbed him by the hair and jerked his head back.

"You said Crestley was mine to do with as I pleased." She looked at him for a long moment. "Please sign that thing, so we can conclude this odious business."

He stared at her, wondering if she was truly trying to signal him that she had a plan, or if she was attempting to trick him into signing. Still, back at Crestley she had trusted him, and he would have to do the same for her. With a snarl he accepted the parchment and pen from DuPres's waiting hand and scribbled his signature. As soon as he had finished, Reid wrenched his arm back behind him and retied the bindings. DuPres lowered the pistol to examine his signature.

"Not your neatest effort, but I believe it will stand up in court," he muttered, folding the parchment.

It would, but only if Nicholas wasn't there to testify that he had been coerced into signing it. "Let Katherine go," he said insistently, wishing he'd had time to think, to leave her something else that could be her own.

"And let Nicholas go," Katherine said, and raised a pistol to aim it at DuPres's chest.

At the back of the warehouse the door was flung open, and Thomas Elder strode into the room. "Kate!" he yelled.

Katherine flinched at the sound, and DuPres leaped toward her. She shrieked and fired the pistol, missing DuPres and nearly taking off Nicholas's head. He ducked reflexively as she let out another scream, kicking Francis in the leg and dodging out of the way.

"Reid!" DuPres bellowed, limping after her, and his henchman ran forward. "Get her!"

"I don't think so," the Viscount of Sheresford returned, launching himself at Reid.

Thomas hadn't let her come alone after all. But Nicholas's relief swiftly turned to dismay as Reid swung a piece of lumber at the viscount and knocked him onto a pile of broken crates. Thomas lurched to his feet and grabbed for the other man. Katherine threw the spent pistol at DuPres and dodged around a pole, trying to work her way back over to Nicholas. She was too damned brave for her own good. Instead of trying to rescue him she should have been heading for the door and safety. Nicholas yanked his arms again, wincing as the movement opened the cuts in his wrists. Shutting his eyes, he yanked again. Hard.

"Your Grace?"

With a start Nicholas opened his eyes. Althaea Hillary stood in front of him. "Miss Hillary. Thank God. Please untie me." She knelt behind him, and he felt her fingers pause as they touched the bloody ropes binding his wrists. To his surprise she didn't faint, but after a moment began to tug at the knots. He wanted to yell at Kate, to tell her to get out while she could, but he didn't want DuPres coming over and stopping Althaea before he was free. He yanked at the ropes again. "Hurry, Miss Hillary."

"I'm trying," she said in her hesitant voice, and went to work again.

"Miss Hillary?"

"Sit still and be quiet. I'm nearly finished," she ordered, tugging hard enough at the bindings to make him wince.

Apparently the flower wasn't as timid as he had thought. Surprised, he complied. After a moment the ropes were loosened and he tugged his hands free. They hurt like hell, but he immediately bent and began pulling at the ropes binding his legs. The last knot came undone, and he staggered to his feet in time to see DuPres grab Katherine by the hair and pull her against him.

"Get your filthy hands off her, DuPres," Nicholas snarled.

"Nicholas," Katherine sobbed, breathless and half hysterical, and punched at DuPres as the madman yanked her toward the door.

Francis pulled his pistol out of his pocket and pointed it at her head, bringing Nicholas to a skidding halt. "Stay right where you are, Sommesby," he said, then bent his head and kissed Katherine wetly on the lips. "It seems I now own several things that used to belong to you," he murmured at the duke, dragging her out the back door and kicking it shut behind him.

"Let go of me!" she shrieked, but DuPres wrenched her arm and pulled her down the alley.

The door was thrown open again behind them, and Francis whipped around, flinging her into the wall. He fired as Nicholas dove behind a pile of rotted cabbage and greens. Katherine couldn't tell whether he had been hit or not, and she screamed again. DuPres grabbed for her, and she ducked away. She yanked the other pistol free from her pocket and aimed it at him. "Leave me alone," she spat out, taking a step backward.

Nicholas lurched to his feet again behind DuPres, who took a step toward her. "Put that down," DuPres ordered.

He lunged forward, and she aimed carefully and pulled the trigger. The shot missed him and dug into the wall a foot in front of Nicholas. "Kate, put that down!" Nicholas bellowed, stumbling again.

DuPres grabbed her arm, wrenching the spent weapon out of her hand and pulling her toward the street. "You'll pay for that, shrew," he snarled.

"Where are you taking me?" she demanded, trying to free her arm and look over her shoulder to see if Nicholas was still behind them. "Nicholas!"

"Shut up. You might think you've ruined things again, but you and I are leaving England for the colonies. I doubt, though, that you'll survive the voyage," DuPres said panting.

That made sense. He would only keep her alive long enough to see that he had gotten safely away from England and the authorities. They reached the street, and he yanked her to the right. His coach stood waiting past the corner and beyond two dozen street vendors and passersby, who all turned to watch them curiously. "I'll kill that bastard Sommesby this time."

"Try it, then."

Nicholas slammed into DuPres from behind, and the two of them crashed onto the cobblestoned street. Katherine stumbled away and threw a hand out against one wall to keep herself from falling. The two men came to their feet at almost the same time, and DuPres slammed the pistol at Nicholas's head. The duke ducked and barreled into the smaller man's chest.

DuPres twisted as he fell and grabbed at Nicholas's ankle, yanking him off his feet. Katherine watched as Francis grabbed the duke around the neck. Varon broke the stranglehold and threw off DuPres. Nicholas dodged sideways and scrambled to his feet, dragging DuPres up with him. While the shorter man punched and kicked at him, screaming curses, Nicholas grabbed him by the back of the collar and slammed his head into the wall. DuPres went limp, but Nicholas did it again. And again.

"Nicholas, stop!"

The duke released his grip and staggered backward. DuPres slid bonelessly to the ground, blood flowing from a deep gash in his forehead. Nicholas straightened and turned toward Katherine. He was bleeding from a cut on his cheek and lip, and dark blood soaked into the right sleeve of his torn jacket.

"Nicholas, are you shot?" she sobbed as she reached his side. He was filthy, his fine jacket torn and muddied.

"A ricochet," he said breathlessly. "Are you all right?"

She nodded, and he wrapped his arms around her, lowering his face into her disheveled hair. "I was afraid I'd lost you," he murmured, pulling her closer. "And we have gone through entirely too much for that." After a moment he leaned away a little and tilted her chin up with his fingers.

"That's the bloody Duke of Sommesby," someone from the crowd called.

"It's the Black Duke," someone else muttered.

Nicholas raised his head and looked around them. "We seem to have attracted an audience," he noted.

"I don't care," Katherine replied, curling her fingers into his jacket. "Take me home, Nicholas," she whispered.

"I will, if you promise never to pick up a firearm again," he muttered, chuckling and keeping his arms close around her.

She gasped, horrified, and touched his arm. "I did this?"

"It's all right, my sweet. You missed me the first time, as it turns out, so I suppose this is only fair."

"What do you mean?"

"It was DuPres."

She looked down at the unconscious figure beside them. "DuPres? How?"

Thomas and Althaea appeared up the street, the viscount shoving Reid in front of him at gunpoint. "I'll explain later." Nicholas released her and bent over to rifle through DuPres's pockets. After a moment he produced the paper he had signed. "Here, this belongs to you."

Katherine looked at it for a moment, then tore it up, letting the pieces flutter down over DuPres's unconscious form. "Now you can have it," she said.

"I'm relieved you had a plan," Nicholas murmured, looking down at her.

She shook her head, stepping forward to rest her head against his shoulder as he hugged her to him again. "I would have let him have Crestley," she whispered, tears starting to form in her eyes, "to save you." Agreeing to relinquish Crestley Hall, given the alternative, had been the easiest decision she had ever made. She would have parted with a hundred Crestleys for Nicholas Varon.

He sighed, his breath warm in her hair. "Thank you," he returned, equally softly. "And I hope to never make you go through that again."

She smiled a little. "I wonder what will go wrong next."

His eyes twinkling, he shook his head. "I really don't wish to take the chance of finding out," he murmured. "You know," he continued softly, touching her cheek, "I think that I fell in love with you the first night we danced."

She eyed him, surprised by the admission and wondering what he was up to now. "But I was awful to you."

"Yes," he agreed, "but very few people are." He gave her a lopsided grin that made her feel weak-kneed. "And now I find that I cannot live without you. I love you, Katherine."

"And I love you, Nicholas," she returned softly, smiling.

"Will you marry me?"

She had never thought to hear him utter those words. "I will."

He closed his eyes for a moment, then opened them again, their emerald highlights glinting at her. "Thank God." He bent his head and kissed her on the lips. She closed her eyes and reached her arms up around his shoulders. His arms enfolded her, and he pulled her tightly against him.

She didn't open her eyes again until their gathering audience began applauding and laughing. "Nicholas," she said, shoving at him and blushing.

"Nick, I'm not certain this is the place for—" Thomas said, his face flushed and a cut bleeding over one eye.

"It's all right, Thomas," the duke replied. "We're to be married." He looked down at her again. "I love you," he whispered.

"And I love you," she returned promptly. "Now let me go."

He shook his head. "Not until you do something for me," he said, his gray eyes dancing.

"What?"

His grin widened wickedly. "Kiss me, Kate, and we will be married on Sunday."

She recognized the reference to *The Taming of the Shrew,* and returned his grin. "We'll wed on Saturday," she improvised.

"And I say 'tis Sunday," he returned.

" 'Tis Saturday," she corrected, and then couldn't argue any longer, because he was kissing her so thoroughly that all she could do was give in and kiss him back while the onlookers cheered the duke and his lady. Black knights were definitely more interesting than white knights, she thought distractedly. And Black Dukes were the best of all.